"I WANT MORE TIME WITH YOU THAN AN HOUR." Gregory still sounded as casual as if they were involved in nothing more than party chatter.

"How much more time?" This time Annabelle gazed at the poster.

The arm around her shoulders became less casual and more purposeful as it tugged her closer. She could feel his warm breath on her ear and the sharp, but pleasant nip of teeth on her earlobe.

"A day?" Her voice was husky.

His free hand brushed tendrils of her hair aside as his lips trailed kisses down her neck. "More," he murmured against her skin.

She turned her face toward his, and the trail of kisses abruptly reversed direction and headed up to the corner of her mouth. He ran the tip of his tongue over her bottom lip, then sucked it gently into his mouth.

"A—a week?" Her voice had become weak, thready, and her head seemed to be floating about twelve inches above her body. "Two weeks?"

"Longer." She could feel his warm breath against her mouth.

"I, ah, don't know." She angled her whole body toward him. "You could . . . mm . . . persuade me. Maybe."

WHAT ARE *LOVESWEPT* ROMANCES?

They are stories of true romance and touching emotion. We believe those two very important ingredients are constants in our highly sensual and very believable stories in the LOVESWEPT *line. Our goal is to give you, the reader, stories of consistently high quality that may sometimes make you laugh, sometimes make you cry, but are always fresh and creative and contain many delightful surprises within their pages.*

Most romance fans read an enormous number of books. Those they truly love, they keep. Others may be traded with friends and soon forgotten. We hope that each LOVESWEPT *romance will be a treasure—a "keeper." We will always try to publish*

LOVE STORIES YOU'LL NEVER FORGET BY AUTHORS YOU'LL ALWAYS REMEMBER

The Editors

Loveswept® 773

THE REBEL AND HIS BRIDE

BONNIE PEGA

BANTAM BOOKS
NEW YORK · TORONTO · LONDON · SYDNEY · AUCKLAND

THE REBEL AND HIS BRIDE

A Bantam Book / January 1996

Bantam Books are published by Bantam Books, a division of Bantam Doubleday Dell Publishing Group, Inc. Its trademark, consisting of the words "Bantam Books" and the portrayal of a rooster, is Registered in U.S. Patent and Trademark Office and in other countries. Marca Registrada. Bantam Books, 1540 Broadway, New York, New York 10036.

PRINTED IN THE UNITED STATES OF AMERICA

OPM   0 9 8 7 6 5 4 3 2

This book is dedicated to all the redheads in my life: my son Scott, my sister Pat Hildebran and her kids Emily, Jane, and Michael.
And to my husband Bill and son Chris who aren't redheads, but shouldn't be left out.

A very special thanks to Leanne Banks for all the pennies (and quarters).

PROLOGUE

Gregory Talbott looked around at the hundreds of students that packed the university commons. The attendance at the Food for Kids rally was better than he'd expected. The other students were enthusiastic and vocal, and he figured the media would show up anytime. He hoped they would get their message across. And maybe while the newspaper and television coverage was going on, he could get in a little free press about the antivivisection demonstration he was planning that weekend at the biology labs.

There were just so many things in the world that needed changing. He intended to tackle them all someday, even though there was hardly enough time in a day to do what he needed to do. Like eat, he thought as his stomach reminded him he hadn't fed it since last night. He spotted a hotdog vendor at the outer edges of the crowd and headed that way. Gregory reached the cart at the same time as a pretty coed with curly pecan-brown hair, a beautiful face, and a slim figure.

"Hey, I only got one wiener left." The vendor held up a shriveled frankfurter.

Even though his stomach growled in protest, Gregory smiled at the woman and offered the hot dog to her. She smiled in return and shook her head, and he thought he'd never seen anything as gorgeous as her smile. It was warm and sunny and crawled right inside him. Yeah, there were a lot of things in the world that needed to be changed, but he wouldn't change that smile for anything.

"Are you sure you won't take it?" he asked.

"No thanks," she said. "You got here a couple of seconds before I did."

Her voice. God, her voice. It was a voice to spin dreams around, a voice that could turn a guy inside out. A voice he wanted to take to a movie Friday night. He turned to the vendor. "I'll take it." He looked back at the woman. "What do you like on your hot dogs? I like catsup."

"I usually take everything."

"Put everything on it," he said to the vendor, though he never took his eyes off the woman. "I'm Gregory Talbott."

"I'm Annabelle Pace. Do your friends call you Greg?"

"They usually call me Talbott. You, however, can call me anything you want."

"I heard you speak at the rally. You're very good."

"Thanks. Wanna bite?" He held up the hot dog.

"I don't bite strange wieners." She grimaced. "I didn't mean that the way it sounded."

Gregory grinned. "I know how you meant it. Does this mean you only bite wieners you know?"

She batted her lashes at him. "I'm sweet and innocent and won't even step on ants on a sidewalk. I don't bite anything."

"Pity. I was hoping."

She rolled her eyes. "Gimme that hot dog."

He held it up to her mouth. She took a bite, but managed to nip the end of his finger in the process. "Ow! You did bite me."

"So I lied. I do bite on occasion."

"God, I love strong women. Go out with me, huh?"

ONE

"So, Preach, what's the cause of the week this week?"

Gregory Talbott stiffened at the all-too-familiar voice. It was the last voice he expected to hear in his church office on a Saturday morning. He hadn't heard it for nine years, but he hadn't forgotten its sweet red velvet texture.

No, he hadn't forgotten the slightest nuance, he thought as he felt the tendrils of past desire pull at him. It took an effort, but he managed to turn his head toward her and say coolly, "Hello, Annabelle. Long time no see."

"It has been a long time, hasn't it, Gregory? Or should I say Reverend Talbott?"

"Gregory's fine." He'd known she'd show up in White Creek sooner or later; after all, she had family here. He wondered briefly if she'd ever told them about her relationship with him. Somehow he didn't think so.

He made himself look at her, really look at her. Long time or not, she hadn't changed much. She looked almost the same as she did when she was nineteen. Or better. Nine years later she still had tousled chestnut curls, only now they were softer and burnished with little streaks of sun-shot gold. She was still slim, but her figure had lost the almost angular slenderness of a girl and had taken on the softer, riper curves of a woman. Her hazel eyes showed the biggest change. The dark gold depths that had once sparkled with eager innocence shone instead with disconcerting maturity.

"When Gran told me you'd taken the church here," she said, "I thought it was a joke. I didn't see how you'd find time to tend a flock between Save the Whale meetings." She perched on the edge of the polished oak desk that had graced the church offices since before World War II. The movement showed off her long gold-tanned legs and slender ankles. It put her breasts right at his eye level.

Gregory moved his gaze up to her chin and gave a weak smile. "What brings you back to White Creek? Did you come because of your grandmother's broken arm?"

She absently ran her finger around the edge of the desk. "I came mostly for that, but I'd have come anyway for Daisy Jones's engagement party in a few weeks."

That drew Gregory's attention away from Annabelle for a moment and he shook his head. It was Daisy's third engagement that year—and it was only June. "You didn't come for the other two."

"The other two didn't last long enough for anyone to worry about an engagement party."

"So," he began, hoping he sounded only casually interested, "how long are you going to be in White Creek?"

"I don't know. I'm going to stay with Gran until the cast comes off. After that, I'm not sure."

"Did Lute Simpson get rid of that motorcycle?"

"After the wreck he and Gran had, he said he wouldn't get back on it if you paid him. He's back driving his pickup."

Gregory nodded and searched for something else to say. "Ah, so what are you doing these days?" He wanted to wince at how lame that sounded, but he couldn't think of anything more dramatic. He could enthrall a Sunday-morning congregation, or so he'd been told, but he could only think of the most mundane comments right now—anything to keep from blurting out what was really on his mind. How could she sit there and look so calm and cool? He felt distinctly frayed around the edges.

"I'm teaching," she answered. "I've taught in Raleigh for the past couple of years, but I'll be teaching this fall at a middle school in Norfolk. Now that Mom and Dad are retiring to Florida to be near my brother and his wife, I want to be closer to Gran."

"Well, family ties are important." Great, he thought, here came the clichés and platitudes. They could always discuss the weather and everybody's health—looks like rain and how's your aunt Gladys's gallbladder? Maybe he'd just shut up and let her think he'd grown more stupid instead of opening his mouth and proving it.

"Well, I expect I'll see you Sunday," she said, hopping down from the desk. She gave an airy wave of her hand and a toss of her head that set her glossy curls bouncing.

"Yeah, Sunday." Gregory watched her walk away. She still had the same boyishly free, long-legged stride that had always captivated him, the sway of her hips accentuated by the snug cutoff jeans she wore.

Seeing her after all these years was like a kick in the stomach—sharp pain followed by an odd breathlessness. She'd been his first serious relationship. At the time he'd thought they'd be together forever. They hadn't made it through his senior year in college.

He almost hoped she wouldn't come to church tomorrow. If he felt this tongue-tied after just five minutes with her, he'd be lucky if he could remember his own name, much less the opening lines to his sermon.

He'd be luckier still if he could keep from grabbing her and shaking out of her the answer to the question that had burned through him all these years.

"Why did you leave me, Annabelle? Why did you leave me?"

"Did you find Daisy at the church?" Virgie Pace, Annabelle's grandmother, looked up from mending her favorite leather jacket as Annabelle entered her house.

"No." Annabelle tossed her purse on the Parsons table in the foyer. Parsons table, she thought with disgust. She couldn't get away from reminders of Gregory.

"I was sure she'd be there," Virgie said. "Why, she said just this morning she was going to check out the—" She stopped, focusing on Annabelle's face. "You certainly look ruffled about something, dear. You ran into the good reverend, didn't you?"

Annabelle sighed and brushed a kiss across the top of her grandmother's bright orange hair. "Oh, I ran into him, all right. I darn near bulldozed over him."

"What happened, honey?" Virgie frowned down at her knee, where she'd accidentally sewn her leather jacket to her jeans. "Darn this cast, anyway."

Annabelle squatted in front of her grandmother. "You just hold still and let me snip the threads."

"What happened between you and the preacher?"

Annabelle sighed. "I jumped down his throat first thing. Self-defense, I suppose. Right now he's probably praying I'll catch the next bus out of here."

"You know I've always hoped that you would manage to put that part of your past behind you. Greg's a good preacher, honey. The best."

A sardonic smile twisted Annabelle's lips just as bitterness twisted her words. "I never doubted that he would be. He'd give it his all—just like he gave his innumerable causes his all. He always gave everything his all—except me. I only got the leftovers."

She clipped the last thread in silence, then told her grandmother she was going to lie down for a while. In her bedroom, she shut the door and flopped down on the bed, hoping the quaintly furnished room would work its magic. She and her cousin Danielle had shared this same bed as children when they'd spent summers here. They'd bounced on the feather mattress, hung their hair ribbons from the brass headboard, and lain on that bed many a night, making girlish wishes and watching the moonlight stream in through the windows.

Now Danni was happily married, expecting twins, sharing a veterinary practice with her husband, Sebastian, and spending two or three weeks each summer doing the traveling she'd always dreamed of. All of her wishes had come true. And Annabelle? Annabelle was hung up on a nine-year-old romance that had gone wrong. Still, she had always felt White Creek and this house were a haven from the rest of the world. She used to come here whenever life overwhelmed her or she had a problem she needed to think through.

Yes, this house had always been a cure for what ailed her. Until Gregory Talbott had accepted the position as minister of the Baptist church six years earlier. She'd only been back once since then, and that had been for Danni and Sebastian's wedding five years ago. Luckily Gregory had been out of town the week of the wedding—an old friend of Sebastian's had officiated at the ceremony—and Annabelle had made darn sure she left the day he was due back.

Out of all the churches in the United States, why had he picked this one? She felt an unreasoning surge of anger at him for invading her turf. This was *her* special place. He had no right to be here!

She sighed and propped her head on her hands. Had it really been nine years since they'd last seen each other? She could have sworn it was just a few weeks, the feelings were still that raw. He looked terrific, she'd noticed that. Time had given him the faintest suggestion of laugh lines at the outer corners of his golden-brown eyes. They gave his face warmth, character.

His copper hair—he'd always referred to it jokingly as the "flames of hell"—was shorter than it used to be. She supposed that was a concession to his job. It still hung down over his collar, though. He'd grown in to the broad shoulders and long legs that used to make him look all bones and angles. Now he just looked good.

She wondered if he still liked to eat roasted peanuts in bed. She used to wake up in the mornings with peanut shells in her hair, but Gregory would brush them out. He used to love playing with her hair, winding the curls around his fingers as he studied.

He had been everything to her. She just hadn't been enough for him. In those days, Gregory had always been looking for a cause to throw himself into. He'd picketed the administration building at the university over student parking. He'd boycotted his science classes for some reason she couldn't remember. He'd gotten thrown in jail during a nuclear-disarmament rally off campus.

She hadn't faulted his causes. How could she when she'd met him at a Food for Kids rally? No, the problem had been that there were no half measures for him. The deeper his involvement with a cause, the more he'd forgotten about everything else—including her. The Saturday he'd picketed the administration building, he had forgotten the afternoon concert he'd promised to take her to. The weekend he'd spent in jail had been the weekend of her sorority's spring formal. And there had been so many other occasions too numerous to count.

A thump next to her on the bed brought her back to the present and she opened her eyes. Merlin, Danni and Sebastian's six-toed cat, had a mouse in tow. He had a nasty habit of catching them and letting them go, unharmed, in strange places. He'd done it at Sebastian and Danni's wedding reception, and the newlyweds had just smiled indulgently. Gran had told Annabelle that last week he'd pulled the same stunt in the middle of Sunday dinner. Gran had laughed about it, but Annabelle thought it was a revolting habit.

This time Merlin walked daintily up to her pillow, sat down with a heavy plop, and let the mouse go. The terrified rodent scurried off the bed and darted across the floor.

Annabelle leaped to her feet. "Don't do that again," she muttered to the cat. "No rodents. Understand? I can't wait till Danni and Sebastian get back and can take you home where you belong. You're weird."

The cat just yawned, blinked his one green eye and one blue eye at her, lifted his hind leg, and began grooming his white stomach. She didn't know how Merlin had gotten into her room through a closed door, and didn't want to know. Danni swore the cat was magic. Maybe he was. Annabelle wasn't in the mood to debate the point.

She had to get out of there, she told herself. She also decided she'd take no more unscheduled trips down memory lane. It was too dangerous. She tugged a brush through her hair and decided to run down to Bosco Wilson's Food Mart and nose around a little. The man carried nearly everything; surely he'd have fudge-swirl ice cream. If Gregory's weakness had been peanuts in the shell, hers was fudge-swirl ice cream. Fudge-swirl ice cream, with crushed praline chips, or strawberries by the quart, had gotten her through many a stressful time. Even though she was now allergic to strawberries, there was nothing stopping her from eating the ice cream. And today was nothing if not a fudge-swirl day.

There was quite a line at Bosco's. The store was closed on Sundays, so just before six o'clock on Saturday night the place bustled with people grabbing the little extras they couldn't live thirty-six hours without. Like fudge-swirl ice cream, Annabelle thought wryly. She snatched a carton and got in line at the checkout stand.

"I see some things haven't changed," Gregory said from right behind her less than half a minute later.

She stopped dead and closed her eyes for a moment. He still had a wonderful voice. It was smooth, mellow, but could rise to dramatic heights. Years ago he had used it to convince people to recycle or to support nuclear disarmament; now he used it to lead people to God. However he used it, she still found it compelling. She pasted on a smile and turned around. "Hello again, Reverend. What hasn't changed?"

"You still love fudge-swirl ice cream."

"I'm just picking this up for Gran."

"Right. And I was just picking these up"—he held up a five-pound bag of peanuts in the shell—"for the board of deacons."

"Do they get the shells in their hair too?" Annabelle snapped her mouth shut, horrified at the words that had slipped out unbidden.

Gregory's smile was disturbingly intimate. "No. That honor was reserved solely for you, Annabelle."

Silence fell for a moment, and she squirmed as the store seemed to get warmer. This was a bad idea, she thought. A really bad idea. After nearly drowning in memories earlier that afternoon, she didn't need to know that he still remembered the way it had been between them. Their relationship had been hot, intense, impassioned. Until other things had gotten in the way.

Was it her imagination or was Gregory's voice huskier when he said, "I'm glad you haven't forgotten. I never have."

Annabelle only wished she could forget. She turned her face toward the front of the store, pretending a great interest in the display of assorted picnic coolers. "I haven't thought much about it," she said, hoping she sounded nonchalant. "I don't know where that comment about the peanut shells came from."

"I used to brush them out for you, remember? I loved brushing them out of your hair." His fingers flexed as if even they hadn't forgotten the feel, and his eyes were dark with memories.

Annabelle sighed. For sanity's sake, it was best to put a quick stop to any more reminiscing. "Gregory, that was long, long ago, in a galaxy far, far away. We're two different people now. Why rehash such old business?"

"We're not so different, Princess Leia." He again lifted his bag of peanuts and nodded at her ice cream.

"This is one of the very few holdovers from my childhood," she said, tilting her chin up. "I've changed a lot in nine years."

"Oh. Well, then, you wouldn't be interested in the jars of crushed praline chips they have here."

Praline chips? Annabelle couldn't help it. Her eyes widened with sudden avarice. "Where?"

"I thought that might get you off your high horse," Gregory said mildly. "I'll tell you where they are if you'll bring the ice cream by the church office and share a dish with me."

"I see preachers aren't above a little petty blackmail sometimes."

"If the occasion warrants it," he drawled. "You should see what lengths I'll go to to enlist new members for the church choir. Do you accept my offer?"

Annabelle hesitated. She knew that was the worst possible idea, but she only had a couple of people in front of her in the line. She looked be-hind Gregory and counted six people. If she got out of line to look for the praline chips herself, the cashier would get to Gregory and he wouldn't be able to save her place. But now that she knew about the praline chips, she just had to have them. She sighed. "Deal. Where are they?"

"The ice cream aisle, on a shelf over the freezer compartment. I'll save your place in line."

Gregory smiled to himself as she dumped the ice cream in his arms and took off toward the back of the store. Annabelle might say she'd changed, but she still loved fudge-swirl ice cream with crushed praline pieces on top.

Without warning a memory slammed into his head of Annabelle sitting cross-legged in his bed, her impossibly wavy hair tousled from their love-making, wearing only his T-shirt and a smile as she offered him a spoonful of ice cream. She said she loved fudge-swirl ice cream better than any-thing else in the whole world—except him—and wouldn't it be wonderful if they could think of some way to combine the two.

It hadn't taken long for them to think of some very creative ways to grant her wish. Gregory felt his body stir at the thoughts going through his head. Not in the store! he admonished himself, and murmured a quick prayer for self-control.

Etta Dawson stopped to chat about the previ-ous Sunday's sermon. He tried to focus his atten-tion on her words, but couldn't keep his eyes off

Annabelle as she walked toward him, a triumphant smile on her lips, the jar of praline chips in her hand. He quickly said, "Mrs. Dawson, I'm sure you've met Annabelle, Virgie Pace's granddaughter."

Mrs. Dawson smiled and murmured a greeting, and Gregory noticed her glance passing from him to Annabelle and back again.

He wanted to groan. Etta was the biggest gossip in the Women's Missionary Society. The society would have him and Annabelle engaged or even married inside of a week all on the basis of a chance meeting at the grocery store. He was used to the gossip—a young single minister would always get his share—but he doubted Annabelle would be amused.

He really didn't want anything to scare her off. At least not before he'd found out what had happened between them so many years ago. Until then, he doubted he'd ever be able to close the door completely on that chapter of his life. Every relationship he'd had, or tried to have, since then had been shadowed by unfinished business.

He'd asked himself many times why Annabelle haunted him so. Was it because she'd been the one true love of his life? Or was it because their relationship had been the most passionate of his life? No one since Annabelle had stirred his libido the way she had.

They each paid for their purchases, although Gregory offered to pay for her ice cream and praline chips too. "Can I give you a ride?" he asked as they walked outside.

"I brought my car."

In the parking lot, Gregory could see her eyes narrow as she perused the bumper stickers plastered all over his 1967 Ford Mustang. Was it the bumper stickers that bothered her or the vehicle itself? It was the same car they used to neck in— before she moved in with him in his tiny off-campus apartment.

"I see that something besides the peanuts hasn't changed either." She indicated his car. "What, no Save the Whale stickers?"

"That's what Greenpeace is for." He indicated their slogan. "They're saving whales these days. I'll see you at the church office?"

She nodded and turned toward her car, but he had her door open for her before she could reach for it.

"Still not locking your car doors," he said.

She shrugged. "Seemed safe enough in Small-Town America. Gran said the last major crime they had here was when Marty Cochran blew up Lute's mailbox. Why'd he do that anyway?"

"One of Lute's goats ate Marty's prize roses. Nevertheless, you can't be too careful. Especially if you're going to be living in Norfolk soon. That's *not* small-town life."

Annabelle shrugged again and got in her car. How familiar this sounded, she thought. Gregory had always been after her to be careful. He'd said she was safeguarding something precious to him and should take better care of it. Apparently, some habits died hard. It frightened her how comfortable it felt to fall back into the old ways.

Her hands tightened on the steering wheel as she followed him out of the parking lot. If she had any sense at all, she'd disregard her promise and head straight back to Gran's. Better yet, straight out of town. However, her curiosity overruled her good sense. She wanted to spend more time with Gregory, to try to reconcile the fiery, passionate young man she'd known with the man he'd become. The preacher he'd become.

She'd often felt jealous of his causes, had thought of them as rivals for his affection. Mistresses. In the ministry, where a congregation demanded everything you had to give, she wondered how he managed—if he managed—to keep his mistresses. Or were they now simply bumper stickers and not the be-all and end-all of his existence? Had his congregation managed to do what she hadn't? Had they managed to give him what he needed to feel complete?

TWO

"Yes, Mrs. Clarke," Gregory said into the phone. "I'll be by the hospital this evening, then . . . I know you're exhausted . . . I'll sit with him a while so you— Yes, I'll be sure to bring my Bible. I know what his favorite passages— Of course, Mrs. Clarke. You've been wonderful to— Yes, tonight, then."

Hanging up the telephone, he turned back to the half-melted dish of ice cream on his desk. He met Annabelle's questioning gaze. "Maurice and Addie Clarke," he explained. "Mo broke his hip in a tractor accident last week and Addie hasn't left his side—much to his dismay, I think. She stays with him every minute and refuses to leave his room unless someone else comes in to sit with him."

"So you graciously volunteer to rescue him from her overzealous attentions?"

"Something like that. Addie means well. She feels it is her Christian duty as a wife to wait on him hand and foot."

"Whether he wants it or not," Annabelle said with a small smile. "The way you say the words *Christian duty* says a lot."

Gregory sighed. "Too many acts of charity are done piously and reluctantly—and often loudly— in the name of Christian duty. Charity should be freely given. And quietly given."

"You mean you should hide your light under a bushel?"

"Too many people set the whole bushel basket on fire." He licked a drop of melted ice cream from the back of his spoon. "Good point for a sermon," he said suddenly, putting his spoon down. He grabbed a pencil and jotted a few quick notes, then looked up at Annabelle with a sheepish expression. "Sorry, but I don't often get ideas for sermons ahead of time. I usually spend the Saturday before stewing over them."

"You always did like to put everything off until the last minute." Her face softened with memories. "I remember one research paper for your environmental studies class, I think it was, that you basically wrote the night before it was due. You finished it about dawn."

Gregory remembered that one too. He'd planned on writing it a week or two ahead of time, but his relationship with Annabelle had been newly serious and he'd been too intrigued with the physical passion between them to think about something as mundane as how to repair the pollution damage to the Chesapeake Bay.

No, intrigued wasn't quite the right word, he thought. Besotted was more like it. He'd been besotted with her, the way her hair had looked spread over his blue-striped pillowcase, the way she'd felt beneath his hands, the way she'd tasted, the little sounds she'd made in the back of her throat when he'd made love to her . . . .

"Gregory?"

He looked up. "What? Oh, sorry. I was lost in thought again."

"Tomorrow's sermon or next week's?"

Neither. His thoughts had been as far from a sermon as they could get. He drew in a deep breath. "Uh, next week's, I think. I've almost finished tomorrow's." He wondered how Annabelle would feel beneath his hands now? There was an enticing new roundness to her curves that fascinated him.

"And about what subject are you going to enlighten us tomorrow?" she asked.

He was careful to keep his gaze above her chin. "Deciding whether or not to ditch church?"

"What, me? I wouldn't miss a chance to see you in your native habitat." She fished the last bit of praline topping from the bottom of her bowl, then stretched out her legs, crossing them at the ankles.

Gregory's gaze locked on her long tanned legs.

Heaven help him, he could remember so vividly the way they would lock around his hips in passion. He lifted his gaze back to her chin, clenching and unclenching his fists before saying evenly, "There's a little ice cream left. Since it's your favorite, do you want it?"

"Oh no. I couldn't eat another bite." She leaned back in her chair, the movement pulling at the buttons on her pink-flowered shirt.

All of Gregory's attention fastened on the tiny bit of white lace visible through the gap in her shirt. A sudden gathering of pressure behind the zipper of his jeans caught him off guard. It had been a long time since he'd felt such unbridled desire—nine years, to be exact. He sent a brief prayer for self-control winging its way upward and opened his mouth to speak. He wasn't sure what he was going to say and could only hope he didn't groan.

Clara Walling, who always came by the church on Saturday evenings to make sure everything was set for Sunday, poked her head in the office. She appeared taken aback to find someone with Gregory, but smiled brightly. "I just put the fresh flowers on the altar, Reverend, and I picked up the bulletins and placed them by the door so the ushers can get to them."

Thank you, Lord, for the distraction. "Thank you, Mrs. Walling. I know I can always count on you to be on top of things."

Mrs. Walling turned a shrewd gaze to Annabelle. "And how are you, dear? I know your grandmother is delighted to have you here in her time of need."

"I'm fine, thanks, Mrs. Walling. And Gran is managing well enough. She only has a broken arm, you know." Annabelle smiled at the older woman, but she wasn't thrilled to see Mrs. Walling, at least not now. She was a well-meaning lady, but she had an earth-mother complex a mile wide.

Childless, she'd proclaimed herself the adopted mother of nearly every child in town—both permanent residents and summer visitors alike. She'd attached herself to Annabelle and Danni when they'd spent summers there as children.

At Danni and Sebastian's wedding five years ago, Mrs. Walling had declared it her duty to see that Annabelle was next to wed. Now, Mrs. Walling's gaze shot from Annabelle to Gregory and back again. Annabelle could almost hear the wheels turning in her head.

"What do you hear from Danielle and Sebastian?" Mrs. Walling asked her.

"They just left on their vacation Friday and should be back before Daisy and Buddy's engagement party."

"Where did they go this year? Last year was Paris, France, I believe."

"Disneyland. They stayed a little closer to home this year to save money for the babies' nursery." Anticipating Mrs. Walling's next question, she added, "They're due the first week in October, if you recall."

Mrs. Walling nodded and said, "Well, I'll just go check on the Communion wafers and leave you two young people to chat. See you in the morning, Reverend."

"Yes, uh, thank you again, Mrs. Walling."

No sooner had Mrs. Walling exited the room than Annabelle was on her feet. "Well, it's been nice, Rev, but I've got to go. See you 'round."

"Uh, Annabelle?" Gregory stood as well. "I'd hoped we could talk a little more." Why couldn't he formulate the words he really wanted to say? Why did they freeze into solid little lumps in the back of his throat? Why couldn't he just say, *How could you leave me, Annabelle?*

"Love to," she said, "but I really do need to go. Gran and Lute are going out tonight and she needs me to help do her hair."

"Oh, sure. I understand. I thought she was managing all right, though."

"Well, she is, but she has trouble doing things that require two hands. Earlier today she was trying to mend the collar on her leather jacket, and ended up sewing it to her blue jeans. And with her arm in a cast, she's hopeless with a curling iron."

Gregory thought fondly of Virgie's bright orange spiked hair and figured she was hopeless with a curling iron even when she had the use of both arms.

"Anyway, I really need to go," Annabelle finished. "See you tomorrow." With a wave she was gone, leaving Gregory looking after her with nine-year-old questions still burning through him. He sat at the desk staring at the almost empty carton of ice cream until long after the remaining few spoonfuls had melted.

She hadn't slept well—partly because she'd lain in bed for hours castigating herself for being such an idiot. It had been the grandmother of all mistakes to eat ice cream with Gregory. And he'd been so charmingly casual about it. Didn't he remember, for God's sake? Didn't he remember? She wished she could forget all the wonderfully wicked and inventive things the two of them used to do with ice cream—and praline chips.

With a quiver of annoyance, she pushed the unwanted memories away. For all her fine talk about no more trips down memory lane, she couldn't seem to stop wallowing in the might-have-beens. When she finally did get to sleep, she tossed and turned through vivid dreams and awoke wondering if it was a sin to fantasize such things about a man of God. The real problem was that he had dared to look at her as if he still thought her attractive.

Merlin jumped up on her bed about five o'clock in the morning, meowed once, and cuddled next to her, his head propped on her shoulder. She thought about her closed bedroom door, wondered briefly how he'd managed to get in, then cuddled him nearer. With the warm comforting body of the cat nestled beside her, she finally managed to fall into a deep, dreamless sleep. The next thing she knew, her grandmother was calling her.

"Annabelle, honey, I thought you were going to church with me this mornin'. It's after nine."

Annabelle's eyes flew open and her feet hit the floor almost simultaneously. She'd overslept! "Uh, yes, Gran. I'll be ready shortly," she called back, pushing her hair out of her face.

"You won't have time for breakfast," her grandmother warned.

"Feed mine to Merlin."

"He's already had his Cheerios," Virgie said, her voice fading as she went on down the hall.

Annabelle shook her head at the cat's odd diet. She doubted he'd eaten regular cat food once in his entire life. Even Sebastian and Danni, who were always admonishing their patients' owners that pet food was for pets and people food for people, fed Merlin portions of whatever they had for meals. Just last night, Annabelle had seen him scarf down some of the applesauce with cinnamon she'd had for a late-night snack.

Weird cat, she thought, and glanced at where he'd curled up in the hollow she'd left in her pillow. Shaking her head, she yawned, rubbed her eyes, and gazed at her reflection in the mirror opposite the bed. After such restless sleep, her curly hair looked like a Brillo pad and she had pillowcase creases on her cheek. *Well, Reverend Talbott,* she thought, *let's see if you still find me attractive this morning.*

She had intended to wear a demure navy suit and pink blouse to church, but in a moment of perversity, she tossed aside the blouse and pulled on a red silk shell with a scoop neck instead. She even rolled the waistband of her skirt over to raise the hem by a couple of inches.

The cat interrupted his morning bath to watch her, and she shot him a defensive look. "I'm not doing this to attract his attention. I'm doing this—" Why? she asked herself. To prove that she still had great-looking legs even though she was two years shy of thirty? To see if Gregory donned a veil of stuffy conservatism with his ministerial robes? To see if she could tease his attention away from his duties?

Sighing, she tugged her skirt back to its original length, but defiantly left on the red shell. And it wasn't because Gregory had always liked her in red. Just to make that point clear, she said as much to the cat. He simply blinked his mismatched eyes and resumed his grooming.

When she arrived at church, she was immediately surrounded by old childhood friends. She and Danni had spent many a summer in White Creek playing with Magda's daughters. Magda, a self-proclaimed Gypsy and owner of several dozen cats, had raised five daughters alone. Her husband, a navy captain, had died twenty-five years before.

Annabelle and Danni had been especially close with the triplets—Rose, Daisy, and Lily—because the triplets were the same age as they were. But they'd also been friends with Anne and Caterina despite the fact that they were one year older and two years younger respectively.

Rose, Lily, and Anne had left White Creek for Norfolk, though they usually showed up on Sunday mornings to attend church and eat Sunday dinner together. Caterina had stayed in town and opened a children's clothing shop, and Daisy had stayed on as a nurse-midwife. They'd kept in touch with Annabelle and Danni via phone calls, letters, and the occasional visit. It was good to see them now, although Daisy wasn't there. She'd overslept, Caterina said. Annabelle was grateful for their presence, hoping it would insulate her from Gregory.

Thirty minutes into the church service she knew that theory was shot all to hell. Heck, she corrected herself as she remembered where she was. She stifled a sigh. A six-foot-thick brick wall probably couldn't insulate her from Gregory. He radiated an energy that drew her, nine years ago and now.

And his voice, she thought. As long as she lived she doubted she'd ever forget his voice. If the laws of physics altered to allow sandpaper to be made of velvet, that would be his voice. Maturity had added a depth and resonance that made it more compelling than ever. His voice was intimate and personal one minute, soaring to the rafters the next, and she was alternately thrilled by it and horrified at being thrilled by it. She found herself hanging on every word but couldn't have told anyone what he'd said.

He looked so remote in his robes. So grown up. So—so preacherlike. Mentally she contrasted that image with the college senior who'd lived in blue jeans and a Greenpeace T-shirt. She missed the college senior. While he might have always been up to his eyeballs in one cause or another, at least he'd been less complex, easier to read. But, in all honesty, maybe she'd been easier to read back then too. After all, she had wanted nothing more than to be the number-one thing in Gregory's life.

With a start, she realized that everyone around her was getting to their feet. Was the service over already? Before she could reach for her purse, she noticed Lily and Caterina opening their hymnals. She turned to Rose to share hers and met a sympathetic smile. "You okay?" Rose whispered. Annabelle nodded.

The triplets knew all about Gregory and Annabelle's deep, dark history. It was okay that they knew, Annabelle thought, but she hoped no one else did. From Danni, she'd already heard about the determination on the part of most of the ladies in town to play matchmaker between Gregory and anybody. They'd apparently been thrusting daughters and nieces and their friends' daughters and nieces at him for the last six years, though to no avail. If the women found out about Gregory and

Annabelle's previous romance, she just knew they'd start rubbing their hands together with glee.

Irritated with herself, she pulled her thoughts back front and center, composing herself as she remained standing for the final benediction. She looked around, her gaze lighting on the side exit, and she decided to head in that direction. No way did she want to get caught in the crush of people milling down the center aisle toward the back to shake hands with the minister. Before she could move, however, she found herself boxed in by Clara Walling, her grandmother, and Bosco Wilson's wife, Elsie.

Annabelle eyed her grandmother's bright perky smile. She'd learned that the brighter her grandmother's smile, the more likely the possibility that she had mischief up her sleeve. She turned to Mrs. Walling. "Hello, Mrs. Walling, it's nice to see you again. Mrs. Wilson, I know I haven't had a chance to visit yet, but I ran into Buddy when I was looking for Daisy yesterday."

Mrs. Wilson's round, weathered face split into a smile. "It's so good you're back in town for a while, Annabelle. I know how much your grandmother misses you. I understand you're an English teacher, aren't you?"

"Um, yes, I am." Annabelle was puzzled by the remark, but from the expression on her grandmother's face, she knew there was a reason behind all this. She couldn't wait to find out what it was.

She gave her grandmother's face another speculative glance. Then again, maybe she could.

Mrs. Walling smiled at Annabelle. "Virgie said that you'd taken charge of the sixth- and seventh-grade plays at the private school you taught at in Raleigh."

Still mystified, Annabelle nodded. "Yes, I worked with the kids on a couple of plays."

"You enjoyed doing it too," her grandmother added.

"Sure, I enjoyed it. Kids are enormously fun to work with."

Mrs. Wilson beamed. "Wonderful. Then, while you're here with your grandmother, I'm sure you wouldn't mind helping with the church's Independence Day play. It's just a couple of hours two nights a week and Saturday afternoons. The play will be presented at the church on the Sunday after Independence Day."

"What?" Annabelle said. Hang around the church, and Gregory, two evenings a week until then? No way! She thought this with such force that she was afraid she might have said it aloud, but apparently not, for the expressions on the faces of the three ladies never changed. "But I can't. I— Gran needs me to help her—"

"Not at all, dear," Virgie said. "Not at all. I'm sure I could spare you. I don't need a baby-sitter, you know. Just a little help around the house on occasion."

Annabelle shot her grandmother a pleading look. "But, Gran—"

"I know how much you'd love to help out, dear, so don't mind me. I'll be happy knowing you're enjoying something so much."

Annabelle acquiesced gracefully, though she gave Virgie a look that promised plenty of argument later. The icing on the cake was her grandmother's hand all but pushing her down the aisle to the back of the church.

"You can't leave without letting the good reverend know what a wonderful sermon he gave this morning," Virgie said. "You know, Annabelle, since he's been here, I haven't dozed off in church even once. I used to sleep through half of Pastor Charles's sermons. Of course, everyone else did too. I remember once—"

Annabelle tuned out the rest of her grandmother's chatter, her attention captured by the tall robed man she was rapidly approaching. She tried sticking out her hand with a hearty "Great sermon, Rev," but he spoiled her quick getaway plan by holding on to her hand far longer than was necessary.

"I'm so glad you made it this morning, Annabelle." His gaze fastened on the neck of her red shell with an intensity any preacher should have had the decency to be ashamed of. Apparently he wasn't, for he looked up and met her eyes with a smile. "And might I say you look especially nice this morning? I've always thought you looked good in red."

She glanced down and saw the tip of a tennis shoe poking out from beneath his severe black robe. For a second she wanted to smile at him, laugh with him, then she regained her sanity and all but jerked her hand from his grasp. "Thanks. See you. Come on, Gran. We need to be going."

"Wait a minute, dear." Virgie shook Gregory's hand. "I'll be expecting you as usual for dinner. I cooked a beautiful roast yesterday afternoon and I've got some scalloped potatoes just ready to pop in the oven when we get home."

"You know I'd never miss one of your home-cooked meals. The way you cook is truly a gift, Virgie." He turned those wicked preacher's eyes back to Annabelle. "And I'm looking forward to sharing a meal with you again, Annabelle. It's been a long time."

No way would she taste a bite of dinner if she had to look at him over the table, she fumed as she drove back to the house. Not only that, but she doubted she'd be able to swallow without something sticking in her throat. She tightened her grip on the steering wheel. She'd be damned—darned—if she'd let him ruin one of her grandmother's meals. He was right about one thing, though. Gran's cooking was truly a gift.

She had to admit that roast beef, scalloped potatoes, and stewed tomatoes would be one of the fancier meals she'd ever shared with Gregory.

Most of their meals together had been fast food consumed in Gregory's tiny apartment. Their first meal together had been one overcooked hot dog at a Feed the Kids rally. Gregory had taken the wiener, then offered her the first bite. They'd been nearly inseparable after that.

If she could choke down one tough blackened wiener, she certainly ought to be able to serve up fork-tender roast beef. She glanced at her grandmother, who was admiring the signatures she'd garnered on her cast. She also wouldn't mind serving up her grandmother's head on a silver platter. "Gran, I'd like a straight answer, please. I want to know what you were doing back there at church. You cornered me into doing that darn play knowing full well it would be throwing me right under Gregory's heels for the next couple of weeks."

Her grandmother flashed an innocent smile, which didn't fool Annabelle for a minute.

"I'm sorry, dear, I didn't realize," she said easily. "I was just thinking how much you'd enjoy having something to occupy your evenings rather than sitting at home with a doddering old lady."

Annabelle snorted. "You're about as doddering as I am, Gran, so don't hand me that. Not many seventy-year-old grandmothers break their arms because they were doing wheelies on a motorcycle with their boyfriends. And at twenty miles over the posted speed limit!"

"We were only ten miles over the speed limit," Virgie protested mildly.

"No sidetracking me, Gran. Why are you deliberately throwing me at Gregory's head?"

"You just said I was tossing you under his heels. Make up your mind, dear." Virgie paused to roll down her window. "But I do think if you spend a bit of time with him, maybe you'll get used to seeing him around and you won't spend so much time away from here."

That last part rang so true that Annabelle fell silent. Was that what she'd been doing? She supposed it was. She had been back to White Creek only once in all the time Gregory had been here. She'd called her grandmother often, and had always spent time with her when she came to Raleigh to visit Annabelle's parents, but Annabelle had stayed away from White Creek. Still, she had a feeling that wasn't the only reason Gran was setting this up. "Are you sure that's all?" she asked suspiciously.

"Would I lie to you, dear?"

Annabelle sighed. Gran would lie to Saint Peter if she thought the reason was a good one. And she'd do it so sweetly, she doubted he'd even mind.

THREE

At least the Gregory who showed up at two for dinner was closer to a Gregory she recognized, rather than the dignified one who wore ministerial robes. This Gregory wore comfortable blue jeans and a white shirt unbuttoned at the throat. He did carry a coat and tie with him—for Sunday-afternoon visits, he said.

Great, Annabelle thought. At least he wouldn't be there all afternoon. Surely she could handle an hour or two of his company, and after all, it wasn't like she'd be alone with him. Gran would be there. Lute Simpson, her grandmother's steady boyfriend for the past five years, would be there, and probably one or two others. It seemed half the town dropped by Gran's for Sunday afternoon dinner at some time or another. Annabelle found herself wishing they'd all make it today. The more the merrier. Or, at least, the more distractions, the better.

It irked her that she wasn't able to simply consign Gregory to old business. But maybe it was hard to do that with your first lover. Particularly if he'd been your only lover. Not that she'd pined away for him for nine years, she told herself. It's just that she'd been too busy to get intimately involved with anyone else. And it wasn't like there hadn't been offers. Just from no one she considered special.

Annabelle muttered a brief hello to Gregory, then headed for the kitchen, saying there were a few last-minute details to take care of. The stewed-tomato and the scalloped-potato casseroles didn't need any diligent attention as they bubbled in the oven, but it was as good an excuse as any to avoid going back into the living room.

She could hear muffled laughter from the other room, Gregory's hearty laugh soaring over everyone else's. His laugh had always been full of energy and contagious good humor, and for a moment she forgot herself and started to smile.

Before the smile could fully form, it was chased away by a surge of anger at Gregory for barging back into her life. For holding her prisoner in her grandmother's house. That was quickly followed by frustration with herself for allowing her feelings about Gregory to prevent her from doing anything she wanted to do. Blast the man, anyway! She'd go in the living room if she darn well pleased, and her feelings about Gregory had nothing to do with anything. They were ancient history. Prehistoric.

Nervously, she swiped her hands down the front of the white trousers she'd changed into and smoothed her tousled curls. After pasting a smile on her face, she walked into the living room and perched on the chair next to Lem Petrie, a grizzled-faced man who could have been anywhere between sixty and ninety. He was a widower whose pride and joy, besides several grandchildren, were his horses, Sally and Pepper. Annabelle asked him about his horses because she knew he'd be content to rattle on for hours, leaving her free to try to ignore the almost physical sensation of Gregory's golden-brown gaze on her.

How could he manage to hold intelligible conversations with both Lute and her grandmother while making her feel that she was the center of his undivided attention? Every time she looked up, she found his gaze still on her—by turns heated, quizzical, curious, frustrated. It took all her concentration to pay attention to what Lem was telling her. She kept wanting to spin around and yell at Gregory to keep his snoopy little eyes to himself.

When the timer sounded in the kitchen, she gratefully leaped to her feet. "I'll get everything ready, Gran. You just relax." She hurried into the kitchen, glad to be alone for a moment to shake off the lingering sensation of Gregory's gaze. She removed the potatoes from the oven and set them on the counter, then started to do the same with the stewed tomatoes. This time, though, she nearly hit Gregory when he walked up behind her.

Startled, she tilted the casserole dish, sloshing some of the contents on the floor. Without thinking, she grabbed the dish with her other hand to steady it, burning her palm in the process. "Ouch!" She hurriedly set down the dish and raised her left hand to peer at it. "Look what you made me do," she snapped irritably.

"Let me take a look," Gregory said, reaching for her hand.

She cradled it close and turned to one side. "It's fine."

"Let me see," he said again, and took her hand in his. He gently turned it over and looked at the pinkened patch on her palm, then turned on the faucet and held her hand under the cool water. "I'm sorry, Annabelle. I didn't mean to startle you," he murmured, all the while rubbing his fingers over the back of her hand.

She tried to remove her hand from his grasp, but Gregory didn't want to let it go. It had been so long since he had touched her. Even this contact, as innocent as it was, brought back so many memories that appeared to have been waiting just beneath the edges of his consciousness. Now they sprang forward and he nearly reeled at their assault.

Almost without his realizing it, his thumb discovered the sensitive skin between her thumb and forefinger and began a circular caress. The skin there was so soft, he thought, but not as soft as her lips had been. Nor as soft as her breasts. And nowhere near as soft as the inside of her thighs. Was she still as soft? He ached with the desire to find out.

He wanted to groan at the intensity of the feelings that swept over him—both the emotional ones and their physical side effects. Closing his eyes for a moment, he wished, hoped, prayed for strength, then opened his eyes and met her gaze. He saw in her expression all the heated memories that were scorching him. "Annabelle—" His voice was so hoarse, it startled him into silence.

Virgie poked her head into the kitchen. "What's goin' on in here, you two? You could've set the table twice over by now."

Annabelle jerked her hand from Gregory's and blotted her damp fingers on a dish towel. "Nothing. I burned my hand a little, but it's okay. I'm just pouring the tea." She ducked her head and set about filling the glasses on the counter with ice.

Gregory wanted to pound his fists on the wall. So close. He'd been so close. For a moment the words he'd been waiting to ask her had hovered on the tip of his tongue. Before he could get them out, though, the interruption had changed everything. Still, he intended to find out just why Annabelle had left him all those years ago. He needed to find out.

All he'd gotten nine years ago was a terse note telling him that it just wasn't working out for her and she was moving back in with her old roommate, Denise. When Gregory had driven to Denise's to see Annabelle, Denise had said she wasn't there, but wouldn't tell him where she was. When he'd called her, she wouldn't come to the phone. He'd even taken to waiting outside her classes, waiting for her to emerge. But when she had, she'd refused to discuss it.

For nine years the only answer he'd had to "Why?" was "It just wasn't working out." Before Annabelle left White Creek, he meant to find out the truth.

"It's a conspiracy!" Annabelle muttered to the cat who was sprawled on her bed. She sat down on the edge of the mattress, craving a moment's respite from the disturbing man in the living room.

Right after dinner, Lem had stood, thanked them for the dinner, and said he was taking his poor ol' arthritic knees for a walk. Lute and Gran had left almost immediately after that, saying they were going to drop in on Magda to chat about Daisy's wedding preparations. Subtlety had never been her grandmother's strong point. It was painfully obvious she was trying to give Annabelle and Gregory privacy.

"Okay," Annabelle said to herself. "All I have to do is remind him he's got visits to make and tell him I'll take care of the dishes. Most men would be glad to escape kitchen duty, anyway." She nodded and got to her feet. With any luck at all, it would work and Gregory would leave.

Apparently she didn't have any luck because Gregory said, "I couldn't leave you to handle all this by yourself. I'll help. I don't mind at all. As a matter of fact, Sebastian and I usually take turns doing cleanup."

"I'll do them," she reiterated firmly. "You're a guest."

"I eat here almost every Sunday, Annabelle. I'm no more a guest than you are. Besides, you have that burn on your hand and shouldn't be sticking it in hot dishwater. As a matter of fact, why don't you let me put some ointment on it and bandage it for you?"

"I don't need any ointment, my hand's much better. And you said you had to visit—"

"I've got plenty of time. I don't need to be at the hospital in Norfolk until five to visit Mo Clarke."

Five? Oh, help, Annabelle thought. She didn't know why being alone with Gregory disturbed her so much, she just knew that it did. And it wasn't just being alone with him, it was the very *idea* of being alone with him. The whole thing was silly, she told herself. She didn't even know him anymore. She'd been in love with a boy. Intense, fiery, passionate, but a boy nonetheless. He was all grown up now and probably didn't bear any resemblance to the boy she'd known. She was sure he was totally different now.

And yet, as the afternoon wore on and they cleared the table and did the dishes together, she kept seeing flashes of the old Gregory beneath the grown-up surface. Who had said, "The more things change, the more they stay the same"? she wondered.

It was strange to see hauntingly familiar glimpses of the boy she'd known. Strange and disconcerting. It was strange to see Gregory's open boyish grin on a man's angular face. Disconcerting to see the golden-brown eyes that had shared so many intimate glances with her now gazing at her with the warm appreciation of a man.

Still, she found herself relaxing as their conversation gradually became less stilted. They even discussed old times—the more innocent ones, anyway—and mutual friends. As she dried a dish he'd handed her she asked, "So whatever happened to Joe Matthews, anyway? The last I heard of him, he was head over heels in love with an animal-rights activist and had gotten thrown into jail with her for helping with a lab break-in somewhere in northern Virginia. Do you know how long they spent in jail?"

To her surprise, Gregory flushed and concentrated on the plate he was washing as if it were expensive china instead of department-store stoneware. "Not long. We—they were released the next day."

Annabelle's eyebrows rose until they met the

wispy strands of hair that fell over her forehead. "We? *You* were involved?"

He sighed. "I was arrested too."

"But this was just, what, about six years ago? You were already a minister by then, weren't you?"

"I was."

"Didn't you get in trouble?"

He was silent for a moment. "The powers-that-be weren't exactly pleased. Neither was the congregation of my first church."

"What happened?"

"It was a nice, but very conservative church in northern Virginia. They asked me to resign. I did. It was as simple as that. Next stop, White Creek."

"But I don't think there's anything more strait-laced than a small town. I can't imagine the people here not minding if their preacher gets thrown in jail. Even if the cause is a good one."

"The people here can be a little conservative, but they're also honest enough to be themselves— and to allow me to be myself. They actually seem to like that I stand up for what I believe."

Annabelle had always liked that about him too. It was just that in standing up for his causes, he'd sometimes forgotten to stand *by* her.

"And," he added, "it's not like I'm the only slightly unconventional one in town, you know."

She had to give him that. Gregory looked posi-tively tame next to corncob-pipe-smoking Magda, who swore she was a Gypsy, and Lute and her or-ange-haired grandmother doing wheelies on motorcycles, and even Sebastian, whom Danni swore could talk to animals. White Creek, for all its small-town conventionality, was remarkably accepting of idiosyncrasies.

Annabelle looked at her watch. "It's about four twenty-five. How long will it take you to get to the hospital?"

"It'll take about thirty minutes, so I guess I'd better go."

"Thanks for helping with the dishes." She dried her hands on a gaily embroidered dish towel, wincing when she rubbed her still-tender palm.

Gregory took her hand again. "I'm sorry, Annabelle." His eyes were solemn.

"It's okay. It hardly hurts now."

"I don't like the idea of you hurting at all," he said softly.

What about all those times I used to hurt and you weren't there? Whenever I needed you, you were always involved in something else. She didn't say those things out loud, but wondered if some remnant of her old hurt showed on her face, because Gregory reached out and ran the fingers of his free hand over her cheek.

"I can't stand the thought of you in pain," he said.

God, he sounded so sincere, like he truly meant it. "I—it's okay. Really."

"I'd feel better if you'd let me put some ointment on it before I go," he murmured, but he wasn't looking at her palm. Instead, his gaze was fastened with heated intensity on her lips.

"It's not necessary," she said, wishing she could take a deep breath. She couldn't seem to look away from his eyes, so like the eyes of the boy, yet so different. The past was getting all confused with the present, she thought just before his lips covered hers and the confusion disappeared.

It didn't matter whether the feelings were current or ancient. What mattered was the hot, slick pressure of his mouth on hers and the warmth of his hand on her cheek. His other hand rested at her waist, and she could feel it through the fabric of her blouse as acutely as if it were bare skin he touched. The languor that overtook her and made her clutch at him for support was both familiar and achingly new.

As Annabelle's soft body melted into his, Gregory groaned and slid both arms around her to hold her close. He tore his lips from hers to draw in a ragged breath, then buried his face in her hair. For one sweet tormented moment he could feel her breasts pressing against his chest, her heart beating next to his, then he felt the breath that shuddered through her and the ever-so-slight stiffening of her back.

Still he wasn't prepared when she pulled away, schooled her face into cool politeness, and made a point of looking at her watch again. "You're going to be late, Rev." The only indication that she was as affected as he, was the barest tremor in her voice.

"Annabelle—"

"I'll get your coat and tie." She spun on her heel and left the room.

Gregory ran a hand through his hair, shaping it into auburn spikes. "Damn!" he muttered, then glanced up and said a quick "Sorry."

Annabelle shoved his coat and tie at him and was holding open the front door while he was still struggling with the passion that had ripped through him just moments before. "See ya," she said, and shut the door behind him.

As Gregory headed his car toward Norfolk he figured he'd better pray for patience. The good Lord had to know it was going to take bucketloads of it to deal with Annabelle.

Mid-June in White Creek was usually warm and a little on the humid side, but Tuesday dawned downright hot and grew hotter as the day wore on. When Annabelle pulled up in front of the church that evening, it hadn't cooled down a bit, even though it was seven o'clock. Thank heaven the church was air-conditioned, she thought, or the play rehearsal would have been miserable.

Will be miserable, she corrected herself when she noticed all the church windows were wide-open. To heck with conventions, she decided, and managed to shimmy out of her panty hose. She undid another button at the neck of her blouse, then fished around in the bottom of her purse until she found a rubber band so she could fasten her hair in a ponytail. Maybe now she wouldn't die from the heat, she'd only pass out.

Several fans were placed around the sanctuary stirring the hot air, and a dozen or so children ranging between the ages of six and twelve milled around the front while Elsie Wilson watched them. Smiling, Annabelle walked in and called out a cheery, "Hi, I'm Annabelle."

The children responded with some shy smiles and hellos and one "Yo, baby," from a freckled nine-year-old boy with an engagingly impudent grin. No sooner had Annabelle set her purse down and removed the script she'd tucked inside than Mrs. Wilson said, "I need to get back to the Food Mart so Buddy can make his date with Daisy. I'm sure you'll manage just fine." She handed Annabelle a stack of papers. "Here are some extra copies of the children's scripts."

Annabelle smiled ruefully. So this was what Elsie Wilson and Clara Walling had meant when they'd said "help out."

"Okay, guys," she said to the children after Mrs. Wilson left, "it's going to take a little while for me to learn everybody's names, so bear with me. Now, let me see what we've got here. Can I have George Washington, Thomas Jefferson, Patrick Henry, and Paul Revere here on my right, the militia on my left, and Martha Washington and Betsy Ross right here?"

She began going over the play with the children, pausing occasionally to fan herself with her script or blot the perspiration from her forehead with a tissue. The children, typically, didn't seem to mind the heat, but after about an hour and a half, their attention began to wander. Suddenly she saw smiles light up their faces. She didn't need to turn around to know it was Gregory. She could feel that irksome gaze of his on the back of her neck.

She watched as he greeted the kids. They seemed at ease with him and he had a special word for each of them. One thing she'd learned as a teacher was that you had more success dealing with children if you treated them with respect and gave them credit for knowing a few home truths. This was something a lot of adults had trouble realizing. Not Gregory. He seemed to know instinctively how to speak *to* kids, not at them. What a wonderful father he'd be, she found herself thinking, and hurriedly pushed the thought away.

As Gregory continued talking with the kids, Annabelle could see a special gleam in the eyes of the four girls involved in the play. Apparently even the youngest of the female gender were not immune to his charms. But she was, she told herself. She was.

"You kids go back to your rehearsal," Gregory said as he ruffled the hair of six-year-old Emmy

Tanner. "I'm just going to go over here and rattle the cage of the air-conditioner monkey to see if I can get him to go back to work."

"Bribe him with a bunch of bananas for me," Annabelle muttered as she again blotted her forehead with a tissue already damp with perspiration.

"Can't take the heat?" Gregory asked, and hoisted a worn leather tool belt.

"I love the heat," she said. "I just love it the most when it's air-conditioned."

They rehearsed another twenty minutes, then the parents showed up to take the children home, except for the Wainscott boys, who lived across the street from the church. Gregory walked to the front door and watched until they'd crossed the street and scampered up their sidewalk. Turning back, he saw Annabelle standing behind him, her purse strap over her shoulder and her car keys in her hand.

"Leaving so soon?" he asked dryly.

"Um, yeah. I don't want to leave Gran alone too long."

"Annabelle, it's not like she's bedridden or anything. If there's a problem, I'm sure she can pick up the phone with her good arm and make a phone call. Maybe she could even stand on her two perfectly good legs and run for help. And knowing Virgie like I do, she'd probably hit an intruder over the head with her cast and lecture him until he felt so guilty he'd turn himself in."

Annabelle smiled. "You're probably right, but I have things I need to do."

"Wash your hair? Wash out silky red blouses like the one you wore Sunday?" He smiled, too, and his gaze held a definite challenge. "One would think you're trying to avoid me, Annabelle."

"Not at all," she said quickly. "I just know you have things to do as well, and I'll let you get to them."

"I could use your help."

"I don't know what I could possibly do. I don't know a thing about writing sermons or picking out next Sunday's hymns."

"Actually I could use your help with the air conditioner."

"I know even less about those."

"I'm trying to put the compressor back in and just need an extra pair of hands for a few minutes." He sighed. "You can do that, can't you? For the sake of all those poor souls who'll be frying at tomorrow night's choir practice if I don't get it fixed?"

"Why don't you call a repairman?"

"It's not in the church budget."

"And I don't suppose you can just request a few dollars at the drop of a hat."

"This is a rural community, with small farms and small businesses. The people in the congregation give what they can financially, and what they can't, they make up for by giving their time. In the long run, that's really what matters."

Annabelle nodded, and he went on.

"There's never a lot of money, but when the church needs painting, it gets done. Bosco donates the paint, various members of the congregation donate their time. Clara Walling always makes sure there are flowers on the altar Sunday morning, even if she has to go into her own garden and clip some of her prize dahlias to do it. If a family falls on hard times, the congregation makes sure there's always food on their table and shoes on their kids' feet. You can't ask for much more than that. And if it means I have to be a repairman on occasion, so be it."

She followed Gregory to the corner window, where the air conditioner was lying in pieces. He quickly had everything reassembled and asked her to hold the front piece in place while he tightened the screws that held it on. As she knelt next to him on the floor, she was close enough that he could feel the warmth of her body. He detected the faintest trace of White Shoulders, her favorite scent.

It was odd how evocative an aroma could be. He could remember the light, sweet fragrance of White Shoulders surrounding him as they fell together on his twin bed. He could remember burying his face in her White Shoulders–scented hair as he thrust into her.

He closed his eyes for a moment, willing the memories away. Seeing her this summer was going to kill him. Had he been another man, he would have tried to seduce her back into his arms and love her out of his system. Being a minister, he could only pray. He definitely believed in the power of prayer and prayed often, but never so much as he had since Annabelle came back into his life four days ago.

The prayers were usually full of pleas for patience and self-control. He figured he was going to have to add a plea to make abstinence more bearable. Annabelle reminded him of his humanity, reminded him that beneath his ministerial robes and spiritual leanings, he wasn't only a man of God. He was a man.

FOUR

"Gregory, what's wrong?" Annabelle asked in concern. "You look pale all of a sudden."

"I think it's the heat," he murmured, and forced his attention back to the old piece of equipment he was trying to coax a few more days out of. Yeah, it was the heat, all right. Body heat. He dropped the screwdriver.

"Uh, could you hand me that, please?"

She handed him the tool. "Are you sure you're all right?"

"I'm fine. It's just been a heck of a day. I won't keep you any longer, I'm sure you're anxious to be getting home. I know you've got to wash your hair." He got to his feet and held out his hand to help her up. He watched her brush nonexistent dust from her skirt, then said, "I'll walk you to your car."

"No need, Rev. I'm parked right outside the front door."

"Will you be at the baseball game tomorrow night?" he asked suddenly.

Annabelle blinked, confused by his abrupt question. She knew, of course, that the church had a baseball team, sponsored by the volunteer fire department. She guessed Gregory was the coach. "I guess I'm going," she said. "As I recall, Gran always goes. It's before choir practice, isn't it?"

"Yeah. Wear jeans."

"For what?"

"With Sebastian on vacation we need someone on third base."

"I don't play baseball."

"It's a real simple game," he said dryly. "You hit a small white ball with a stick and run around this field, trying to get back to where you started from before the ball catches up to you."

Annabelle couldn't prevent a smile. "I know how it's played, Gregory. I've just never played."

"Okay, then I'll pull Bill Parker from the outfield and put him at third and you can play right field. Since most batters are right-handed, they tend to hit more balls to left field. You might not have to catch one at all."

Part of her really wanted to do this. She didn't know why, though. "I'm not sure, Gregory."

"Come on, Annabelle. I'd hate for the church to lose by forfeit. It's going to be hard enough to win with Sebastian gone."

"I'm probably not going to be any good."

"Oh, you're a natural. I can tell."

"You'd say that to Gran's pet pig, if necessary, to keep from forfeiting, wouldn't you?"

He smiled. "What can I say? So, tell me, would a bribe work?"

"Try me."

"You play and I'll send over a whole gallon of fudge-swirl ice cream."

"With praline chips?"

"Of course."

"You've got it."

"See you at six, then, at the ball field behind the fire station. You'll be terrific, you'll see."

She hadn't been terrific, Annabelle thought the next evening as she tried to wipe red dirt smears from her jeans. But she hadn't been terrible either. She'd missed a couple of balls hit in her direction, but had made one nice catch. She hadn't hit the ball at all, but had walked twice. All in all, she'd had fun. It had been interesting to watch Gregory too.

He was the coach, as well as the pitcher. He played hard, he played to win, but he played fair. He made sure everyone who turned up for the game had a chance to play, even when they were down by two runs and it was Lem Petrie's turn to bat. Gran said that Lem Petrie couldn't hit a baseball if it hung in midair and waited for him, but Gregory put him in and cheered louder than anyone. And when Lem struck out as usual, Gregory clapped him on the back and good-naturedly grumbled about the umpire's lousy eyesight.

Annabelle realized she would have liked Gregory, had she just met him that day. Part of her wished she had just met him. Still, she found a little—the barest amount—of her emotional armor eroding.

More emotional armor eroded over the next two weeks. Annabelle felt comfortable in White Creek. She liked taking evening strolls with Gran and having neighbors wave and say "Howdy." Even the people she didn't know always seemed to have a kind word and a friendly smile.

In Raleigh, even though her apartment building only held six apartments, she hadn't known any of her neighbors. Not even well enough to speak if they saw each other in the laundry room. She found herself wondering if it would be the same in Norfolk as it had been in Raleigh. Suddenly the idea of living in Norfolk wasn't nearly as appealing.

Norfolk became even less appealing when she thought about leaving Gran. Despite her eccentricities and the streak of mischief a mile wide—or maybe because of them—Annabelle genuinely enjoyed being around her. And she reminded herself that, though Gran might deny it, she wasn't getting any younger.

She toyed with the idea of staying in White

Creek and commuting to Norfolk. That would be nice, she thought wistfully, but she wasn't sure about being around Gregory. Though, she had to admit she'd been able to relax around him recently. On the rare occasions when she was able to forget he was an ex-lover, she even found herself liking him more and more. She liked the easy manner he had with the kids. At the baseball games every Wednesday, she liked his sense of friendly competition and sportsmanship.

It actually got to the point that she was able to sit in the same room with him after Sunday dinner and not feel the urge to flee, or at least it wasn't so overwhelming that she couldn't ignore it. It became a habit for him to show up after play rehearsal—ostensibly to lock up after her—but he usually brought her a cold can of soda and they'd sit on the church porch for a few minutes and chat. Annabelle was careful to stick to talking about the kids and the play.

He seemed friendly and comfortable. Almost. There were still odd moments when she found him watching her with that expression in his eyes that drove her crazy. She sensed that he wanted something from her, but couldn't figure out what it was. Her physical awareness of him was still there, too, but she tried to ignore it. Unfortunately, she wasn't very successful.

After the next-to-the-last rehearsal, Gregory showed up, as usual, right at nine o'clock. He was wearing jeans and an old college sweatshirt with the sleeves cut off. She stared at the sweatshirt, her stomach tight. God, she remembered that shirt. She'd given it to him at Christmas. Their first and only Christmas together.

As soon as the last child had left, she turned to Gregory and said, "You kept it."

He glanced down at the sweatshirt. "You had one like it. Marty accused us of trying to look like the Bobbsey twins when we showed up for the frat's Christmas party both wearing identical sweatshirts and blue jeans."

"And even the same color tennis shoes."

"Yeah. I'd forgotten that."

"I'm just surprised you still have it after all this time."

"I kept everything you ever gave me."

Annabelle fell silent. It was gone, she thought. That comfortable feeling. Chased away with that one sentence and a nine-year-old sweatshirt. The itchy feeling beneath her skin was back, along with the questions in Gregory's eyes. Or maybe the questions had never really gone away and she had been fooling herself into thinking they had.

Time to go home. "I, uh, can't stay to chat tonight. I have things to do."

He nodded and handed her the soda he'd brought. "You may as well take this with you. I have to tinker with that air conditioner again, anyway."

Gregory stood in the doorway and watched Annabelle as she got into her car and drove away.

Sighing heavily, he went back inside the church, hoping to coax a few more gasps of cold air from the cranky air conditioner.

After a few minutes he sank down on the nearest pew and leaned his forehead on his hands. Over the past couple of weeks he had begun to think he might get through Annabelle's prickly exterior. Tonight, though, the prickles seemed to be back. In full force.

Not that it mattered. She was under his skin, as thoroughly as if they'd never been apart. He wished he could say he was happy about it, but the truth was he wasn't sure how he felt. All he knew was that his life had been great until Annabelle came back. Well, okay, maybe not great, he admitted, but certainly fulfilling. And if he hadn't been exactly happy, then at least he'd been satisfied. Until now.

Now she made him realize that no matter how much he loved being a minister and loved the honest, earthy people of White Creek, that didn't make up for the lack in his own life. It didn't make up for the empty house that greeted him at the end of each long day.

When he sat in his cozy little den working on his sermon, it was to the echoes of emptiness all around him. There was no sweet female voice humming in the background—not that Annabelle's voice had ever been sweet, it was too full of sparkle and sass—no high-pitched giggles of children in the distance. There wasn't even the snuffle and sigh of a dog sleeping in the middle of the floor, just the occasional scratchings of Sebastian and Danni's strange cat when he came to visit.

When he pitched for the church baseball team, lots of people cheered him on, but no one special, never anyone special. When he lost a member of his flock, the death always cut him like a knife. He spoke words of comfort to everyone else, but there was no one to comfort him. And when he went to bed and tossed and turned half the night, he could only think it was because he was sleeping alone in a bed meant for two.

He wondered what it would be like to have someone there for him—someone who cared that he'd had an exhausting day, who cared when he hit a home run or had to conduct the funeral for someone who had not only been a member of his congregation, but a valued friend as well.

He lifted his head and stared up at the small chandeliers that had graced the ceiling of the century-old church for fifty years or more. Had he only now realized how empty his personal life was, or had he known it all along and simply tried to convince himself that his work was enough?

With a swipe of his hand through his hair, he slowly got to his feet. He could hardly bear the thought of going home to the little house he'd just admitted was unutterably empty. He glanced at his watch. It was only nine-thirty. Maybe he'd just go upstairs to his church office and sit. And sit. And

stare out the window at the dark night that seemed
to match his mood.

"You've got dirt in your hair."

Gregory spun around. "Annabelle?"

She waved a hand at his head. "You've got
streaks of dirt in your hair."

He looked down at his hands, noting the black
grease stains on them. Fishing a handkerchief out
of his back pocket, he began wiping at the smears.
"I thought you'd gone."

"I left my purse here."

"Oh." Great, he thought. Grab her attention
with your sparkling wit, why don't you?

"I sort of figured you'd be gone by now, but
thought I'd check and see. Don't you ever go
home?"

When there's a reason, he thought. "Uh, yeah.
I just wanted to make sure the air conditioner was
cooling properly."

She raised her eyebrows. "Don't you think you
might want to close the windows first, Rev?"

"Oh, right. I was just getting to that."

A speculative look on her face, Annabelle
watched Gregory as he strode from window to
window, pulling them closed and fastening the
latches. For a moment, when she'd first walked in,
she'd noticed the strangest expression on his face
—lonely, maybe, or sad—and she couldn't help but
wonder what had put that gray bleak look there.

Gregory came back over to her and handed her

the purse she'd left at the front of the church. "Here. I, uh, good night, then."

For some reason she couldn't fathom, Annabelle was suddenly in no hurry to leave, even though she hadn't been able to get out of there fast enough half an hour ago. Maybe it was because she was bored and there was nothing good on television. Or maybe it was because her grandmother had gone to Lute's house to watch rented videos and eat popcorn. And maybe it had something to do with the lingering shadows in Gregory's eyes. She set her purse on the nearest pew and strolled up the center aisle. Gregory followed her.

She stepped up behind the pulpit. "So this is what it's like up here." She glanced down at the small shelves just beneath the podium and pulled out a comic book. "Your secret's out," she said, waving it in the air. "I didn't know you read Galaxy Avenger."

"A lot of things you don't know about me now, Annabelle," he said lightly. "Including my choice of reading material. Though, if I'm not mistaken, Charlie Osgood, the choir director, confiscated that from one of the boys in the junior choir a couple of weeks ago. I guess he forgot to give it back."

She leaned back against the railing that ran the length of the choir loft. "Likely story. So what is your choice of reading material now? It used to be environmental journals."

"Still is. Though I manage to get in a few

sports magazines once in a while and I find time to read the occasional novel."

"What, no *Preacher's Weekly*?"

"Actually, it's *Minister's Quarterly.*"

"Do you still read Tony Hillerman and Tom Clancy?"

He nodded. "And Clive Barker, Dean Koontz."

Annabelle made a tsking sound. "A minister reading horror. Whatever would the board of deacons say?"

Gregory grinned. "Well, they usually ask me to please read faster. They tend to borrow my books. So how about you, Annabelle? You still read science fiction and romance?"

"I do. Though I manage to work in a little Dean Koontz myself, on occasion."

Gregory raised his eyebrows. "*You* reading horror? You couldn't even watch late-night horror movies without hiding your eyes."

"Like I said before, that was long, long ago."

"In a galaxy far, far away. I know. You always did have a thing for *Star Wars.*"

"Maybe it was Harrison Ford I had a thing for. Did you ever think of that?"

"Personally, I always thought it was Darth Vader. Tall, dark, and electronic."

Annabelle's expression softened with memories. "I remember when you dressed up like Darth Vader for that Kappa Delta frat party."

"And you dressed like Princess Leia and spent

the afternoon trying to pin your hair in those big twists over each ear, until Marty suggested you try oversized earmuffs instead."

"And remember when the policeman stopped us because your taillight was out? When he walked up to the car window, he didn't even bat an eye."

Gregory chuckled. "All he said was 'The Empire can't expect to take over the galaxy if it can't keep one measly little car in working order.'"

They both smiled at the shared memory, then Gregory said, "I'm glad you came back tonight. I've been wanting to thank you for taking the time to work on the play with the kids. It would have been too much for Clara Walling and Elsie Wilson to handle, particularly with Buddy getting married soon. Elsie is so distracted with the wedding, and that leaves most of the burden on poor Clara. Besides, I think it's good for the kids to work with a young adult for a change."

"Has that been a problem here? Getting young adults to stay in White Creek, instead of moving to a big city?"

"When I first took over the church here, there seemed to be a mass exodus of anyone between the ages of eighteen and forty, but things are getting better. We've got Danni and Sebastian, Buddy Wilson has decided to stay on and help his father with the Food Mart, Magda's daughter, Caterina, has opened up a children's clothing shop, Lem Petrie's youngest son and his wife have just moved back, and there are others too."

"I'd guess that a lot of people, once they get married and begin thinking about raising a family, move back to small towns, where drug and gang problems are just about nonexistent, and if your kid tries to sneak a cigarette, everyone in town knows."

Gregory studied her. "Have you thought about living in White Creek while you're teaching in Norfolk? It's only forty minutes driving time."

"An hour if the traffic's bad."

"At least the only traffic you'd ever have to worry about is in Norfolk. The last time we had a traffic jam around here was when Joel Harrison's tractor stalled in front of the hardware store and the few cars caught behind him simply drove up on the sidewalk to get around."

Annabelle smiled slightly. "I've thought about staying here. I mean, I know Danni's going to appreciate all the help she can get once she has the twins, particularly since she intends to keep up her part of the veterinary practice. And Gran's not getting any younger, though you'd never know it by her ridiculous shenanigans on Lute's motorcycle."

"Maybe that's the best reason for staying. Your grandmother needs a stable influence in her life. God only knows what she'll get into next. Maybe a tattoo to go with her leather jacket."

"Nothing would surprise me where she's concerned." Annabelle rolled her eyes. "Whatever happened to sweet little old silver-haired grandmas who baked cookies and sang in the church choir?

Danni and I have got to be the only two people in the world to have a biker granny." She sounded irritated, but the twinkle in her eyes said she was more proud than ashamed of her unconventional relative.

Gregory smiled at her unconditional love for her sometimes aggravating, sometimes mischievous, always well-meaning grandmother. "I guess most everybody has one relative or another who's strange. I was the strange one in my family."

"What do you mean?" Annabelle asked.

"I was the only one not aiming for some high-powered career that would rake in the big bucks. One sister is a bank president, the other a corporate attorney. My brother's a doctor. And, of course, Dad and Mom are co-owners of their own software company. They expected me to follow in everyone else's footsteps. They didn't understand years ago when I decided to become a marine biologist. They understood even less when I dropped that and went into the ministry instead."

Annabelle wandered over to the first pew and sat in the corner, stretching her legs out and slipping off her shoes. "So why did you? I mean, you'd always been dead set on getting a job with Greenpeace. I remember when you talked to that guy who worked onboard their ship, *The Rainbow Warrior*, and you'd pretty well decided that's what you wanted to do. Awfully big step from saving whales to saving souls."

Gregory sat next to her. Though he was a respectable distance away, Annabelle found herself feeling crowded by his nearness. The sudden desire for flight again swept over her, but she wanted to hear what he had to say more than she wanted to leave.

"I don't know if I can explain it any better to you than I did to my parents, Annabelle. One morning I woke up and it suddenly occurred to me that all the problems plaguing the environment, all the animal abuse, all the new weapons being developed, were just symptoms of a much bigger problem."

"Which is . . . ?"

"We've lost hope, we've lost compassion." He shook his head. "We've lost faith."

"And so you felt the call to try to restore some of that lost faith."

"Very strongly. Do you understand?"

Her eyes narrowed in thought, then she said slowly, "You know, I think I do. That's one of the reasons teaching means so much to me. Because most kids haven't lost their way yet and maybe all they need is someone to help them find a joy for learning. That's a joy they'll never lose."

Gregory nodded in understanding, and for a moment she felt in tune with him. Just like she used to. Simpatico, their friends had called them.

"So our goals aren't so terribly different, are they?" he said. "I'm out to save souls, you're looking to save minds."

"All we need is your brother the doctor to save

their bodies and we'll have all the bases covered."
Annabelle laughed.

Gregory joined in and, somehow, in the
warmth of shared laughter, their hands touched,
their fingers tangled. Annabelle's laughter died as
abruptly as if someone had pulled a plug, and she
couldn't keep her gaze from lighting on their
joined hands.

Gregory turned her hand over and ran his
thumb across the slight pink patch that was all that
remained of her burn. He raised her hand to his
lips, pressing a soft kiss to the palm. His breath
warm against her skin, he murmured, "The burn
seems better," then looked startled, as if the husky
sound of his voice had surprised him.

"It is." Annabelle tried to retrieve her hand,
but he curled his fingers around hers. It surprised
her how natural it was to nestle her hand in his.
How many times had they walked across campus
hand in hand? How many evenings had they spent
holding hands across a table in the library? And
how many nights had he clasped her hands over
her head, their fingers entwined, as he made passionate love to her?

Gregory released her hand, but only to slide his
hand up her arm to her elbow, cupping it for a
moment, before continuing his journey to her
shoulder. Despite the temperature, which remained in the eighties, gooseflesh appeared on her
arms. His fingers curled into her shoulder, then
slid around to the back of her neck. He toyed with

the tiny curls escaping from her ponytail, winding them around his fingers.

Without thinking, Annabelle ran her tongue over her lips, and saw Gregory fasten his gaze there. He was going to kiss her, she thought with certainty. She couldn't let him kiss her. It would dredge up too many old feelings, feelings that should stay buried. But a delicious lethargy overtook her and she couldn't seem to drum up the energy to move away from him.

He brought up his other hand to cup her face, his thumb tracing her lips. If he had tried to kiss her right then, she could have resisted. But he didn't. When she felt his fingers tracing the shape of her ear, she knew he didn't intend to play fair. No, his plan was insidious. He was going to seduce a kiss from her. And the way he was going about it, he'd get it too.

His fingers lingered on her ear, then trailed slowly down her neck to the small hollow at the base of her throat where an out-of-control pulse fluttered. His fingertips drew little circles there before moving up to her cheek. His touch was deliberate and impetuous, demanding and giving, innocent and passionate.

His head lowered toward hers, but he bypassed her lips in favor of her forehead, her nose, her eyelids. Each kiss was the barest touch, hardly more than the brush of butterfly wings, but it still seemed as if each had the jolt of a thousand volts of electricity.

"I've missed you." The words were so soft, she wasn't sure whether she'd really heard them or merely felt them. When Gregory's lips covered hers a moment later, she no longer cared whether the words came from him—or her. And, still, the only parts of them that touched were their clasped hands, the barest caress of his other hand on her face, and their lips. It was, at one and the same time, far too much and not nearly enough.

Even though she knew it would only complicate her already bewildering feelings for Gregory, she couldn't stop her free hand from sliding behind his head and holding him to her. With a jerky move that showed more need than finesse, he wrapped his arms around her, pulling her close. He slid his tongue along hers, stroking and teasing. Slick, hot, talented.

Gregory had always approached kissing like a sculptor approached a lump of clay, she thought hazily. He had molded each kiss, shaped it, made it his. Oh yes, when it came to kissing he used to be good. Now he was better. She could feel desire curling in her middle, spiraling outward, reaching its molten fingers to tickle every nerve ending.

She was terrified. Terrified he'd stop kissing her. Terrified he'd continue to kiss her. Deep inside, she knew this wasn't a good idea, but she felt powerless to do anything about it. Powerless against the irresistible force of his lips, his arms. She could only weave her fingers through his hair, open her mouth wider to his, melt fully against him. He kissed her as though he were the world's thirstiest man drinking from a cool clear spring. He kissed her as though he'd never get enough.

Her thoughts became fragmented, disjointed. So long, she mused. It had been so long. Her breasts fit against his chest just right, his arms held her just right. No one had ever made her feel the way he had. Her breasts were full and swollen, aching for his touch. She pressed even closer to him, wordlessly, mindlessly.

His hands slid down her shoulders and slipped just beneath the edge of her crop top, his fingers splaying over the bare skin of her back. He'd always been so in tune with her, known just what she needed, wanted, when they made love. And so he knew now. As if he'd read her mind, he moved his hands around to cup her breasts in their lacy covering, his thumbs unerringly finding her rapidly hardening nipples.

She gasped and braced her hands against his chest. She could feel his heartbeat. It thumped hard and fast against her hands. As hard and fast as her own. She could feel the desire that bunched his muscles beneath his shirt, the same desire that whirled through her. She could feel the ragged breaths he drew in as he continued to cradle her breasts in his hands—ragged breaths that she echoed at his touch. And she could feel the sudden deep breath he drew in as he slowly, reluctantly, removed his hands from beneath her shirt.

He pressed one more kiss to her lips, a soft,

sweet kiss, then ran his hands over her shoulders and gently set her away from him. Annabelle couldn't think of anything to say. Apparently he couldn't either, because he just looked at her, searching her face as if looking for the answer to something, to some question only he knew.

"Annabelle—"

She didn't want to hear what he had to say, didn't want to stay there any longer. It wasn't safe for her to be around him. What had happened just a minute before was proof of that. "I've got to go." She jumped to her feet, ran a shaky hand over her hair, and all but ran down the aisle. She paused long enough to grab her purse from the pew where she'd left it and cast one glance back at Gregory. He stood motionless, watching her as though he wasn't surprised at her flight. Without another word, she turned and left.

Gregory gazed after her, long after he'd heard her car pull away. He'd almost gotten the question out that time, would have had she not fled. Frustration joined the heady arousal still humming along his nerve endings, finally replacing it altogether. She was always running away from him. Just as she had nine years ago.

Dammit! He held on to his anger long enough to stride down the aisle of the church and out the door, securing it behind him. When he got into his car, he slammed the door with a satisfying thud, then clenched his fists on the steering wheel. He muttered a quick prayer of apology, then swore violently.

He swore for several minutes straight, long and hard and savagely, though he managed not to take the Lord's name in vain even once. When his anger was spent, he said another prayer apologizing for his lack of self-control. Still he had to admit there seemed to be times when only swearing could adequately express one's feelings—especially when those feelings had to do with Annabelle. Since God had created both man and woman, Gregory had to believe He would surely understand.

He turned the key in the ignition and headed home, wondering if Adam had ever felt this way about Eve. Had he ever had the desire not to just taste the fruit she offered, but to throw it at her?

FIVE

Annabelle woke the next morning bleary-eyed and cross. She also had a crick in her neck from spending most of the night with her head hanging off the bed. At least she assumed that was why her neck hurt—particularly when she met the unblinking gaze of the cat who lay purring on her pillow. Annabelle gave a long-suffering sigh.

This had all the earmarks of a miserable summer. Between a weird cat, a heat wave, and a sinfully sexy minister—who probably had something to do with the heat wave—she was sure she'd be crazy by August. What had possessed her to tell Gran she would stay in White Creek through the summer, rather than just until Gran's cast came off? Sure, she was considering moving back to White Creek for good, and this was an excellent way to find out if the place still suited her. But she was afraid she'd never be able to survive being around Gregory, at least not with her sanity intact. And her heart.

Not only did she still find him desirable, she found him more desirable than she ever had. The man he'd become appealed to the woman she'd become. The icing on the cake was that she *liked* him. She really liked all the new things she was learning about him.

That kiss last night, though, had ruined everything. She'd been able to spend the past couple of weeks on a casually friendly basis with him, carefully glossing over the deeper emotions that ran inside. Their kiss had kicked the facade away and exposed all the raw need and old hurt that still lay beneath.

She spent the morning at home. It felt safer. She did a little housework and helped her grandmother bathe Marigold, her pet pig, in the inflatable wading pool in the backyard.

"So how's the work on the play going?" Virgie asked as she reached for the brush she used to scrub Marigold.

"Gran, I'll do that. You just watch and keep that cast dry."

"Marigold likes to be scrubbed a certain way, honey," Virgie said, though she relinquished the brush. "Use small circles and a firm, but gentle pressure. And work up a good lather. She likes lots of suds." She patted the pig on the head. "Did you see the preacher at church last night?"

As if you didn't know I would! "Mm, yeah," she

murmured. "You know, Gran, I think I'll run out to Magda's later this afternoon. Daisy and I haven't had much of a chance to just sit and talk."

"Did you get along all right?"

She pretended to misunderstand. "Daisy and I get along fine, Gran."

"I mean you and the reverend."

Annabelle gritted her teeth, but kept her expression impassive. "We get along fine, too, Gran. Why shouldn't we? He's a preacher. It's his job to get along with everyone. I'm not sure I remember how to get to Magda's, so you'll need to tell me before I go. I never can remember whether it's the first road after Denning's Creek or the second."

"When do you see him again?"

"See who?" she asked in an innocent voice.

"Why, the reverend, of course."

"How should I know? I may run into him tomorrow night at rehearsal. If not, I'll probably see him on Sunday at church. *If* I decide not to sleep in," she added deliberately, hoping her grandmother was astute enough to hear the exasperation in her voice.

Apparently her grandmother *was* astute enough, because she dropped the subject. Annabelle was grateful for the reprieve, though she knew it was only temporary. But she really didn't want to talk about Gregory. She didn't want to think about him, either. What a shame she could ask her grandmother to drop the subject, but couldn't make her own brain click off.

She worked hard the rest of the day to think of something other than Gregory, and with the distractions posed by her drive out to Magda's, she managed to repair some, though not all, of the chinks in her emotional armor.

She smiled as she drove down the dirt road, riddled with mud puddles, that led to Magda's. She'd always loved this part of White Creek. The long dirt road was bordered on either side by the fields of strawberries that Magda tended. She sold the fruit at a couple of roadside stands over in Waverly, and used the money to help pay for food for the dozens of stray cats she made a home for.

Annabelle could remember spending many a summer afternoon here with Magda's daughters, surrounded by purring cats and stuffed with sweet juicy strawberries. She missed those days, especially since she'd developed an allergy to strawberries about five or six years ago.

When they were teenagers, she and Danni had spent hot summer evenings with the girls giggling over one boy or another. If she remembered correctly, Lily, not Daisy, had had a crush on Buddy Wilson throughout high school.

As she negotiated the potholes in the road Annabelle quickly called a few clichés to mind, in case Daisy wanted to know how she was handling seeing Gregory again. *Honestly, it's fine. We're just good friends now.* No, too vague. *It was over long ago.* The problem was she wasn't sure it was over. *Oh, come on, let's talk about something more interesting—like your love life.* Maybe that one would work.

Unfortunately, no one except the cats were home at Magda's, and Annabelle certainly didn't want to go back to Gran's and stare at the walls. She needed distraction, so she headed farther down the dirt road to Ferndale, Lem Petrie's fancy-sounding, but dilapidated farmhouse. She chatted with Lem a while, admired his horses Sally and Pepper, and left with a bushel basket half-full of baby squash and early cucumbers.

On the way home, she stopped by Caterina's shop and visited, then went by Bosco's and treated herself to a Bosco Sunrise Special—a lemon Sno-Kone with a swirl of orange and a squirt of cherry in the center. She spent a few more minutes chatting with Bosco's mother, Ada, who cashiered for Bosco two days a week.

It took some effort, but she managed to keep her mind off Gregory, even during an evening spent with Gran and Lute watching television. Gran, bless her heart, was more interested in hearing about Lute's drive up to Richmond than in pumping Annabelle for more information about her relationship, such as it was, with Gregory.

By bedtime she was feeling pretty pleased with herself. Every time Gregory's face had popped into her mind during the evening, she'd been able to distract herself long enough to get past it. She wasn't just pleased, she was downright proud of herself. Maybe she'd survive this summer after all.

She should have known, she told herself later, that pride goeth before a fall. Her conscious mind had been moderately successful in not dwelling on Gregory, but her subconscious mind didn't even try to fight it. She couldn't have been asleep long before a vivid dream—a memory, really—swept her back into the past.

Gregory unlocked the door to the tiny one-room apartment he rented off campus. Before he entered, he turned to Annabelle. "Are you sure, babe?"

Annabelle had loved Gregory for nearly all the three months she'd known him, but going to bed with him was still a big step. When she looked into his eyes and saw the tender yearning there, her answer was clear. "I'm sure."

When he closed the door, she burrowed into his arms and he kissed her. She opened her mouth to him, shivering when he deepened the kiss. His kisses had always been a wonderful end to their evenings, but tonight she knew it was just the beginning. She wrapped her arms tighter around him, pressing her suddenly sensitive breasts to his chest.

He pulled back far enough for his gaze to search hers. Apparently satisfied with what he saw, he lowered his head and kissed her again. He kissed her until she pushed away and began to unbutton the denim shirt she wore. Gregory brushed her hands aside and finished the job himself, then drew her shirt down her arms.

She felt her face flush when he unfastened her plain white bra and tossed it aside and she fought the urge to cover herself with her hands. All her self-consciousness disappeared when she saw Gregory's face. He looked at her in awe as he cupped each breast in his hands and groaned. "Beautiful," he murmured. "You're so beautiful."

She felt beautiful as he caressed her breasts, kissed them, sucked the aching tips into his mouth. She also felt things she'd never felt before. She felt as if all the blood coursing through her veins had suddenly pooled low in her body and heated to the boiling point. She whispered his name, but didn't know how to say what she was feeling, didn't know how to ask for what she needed.

Gregory, with flawless intuition, seemed to know. He took her by the hand and led her next to the bed. Instead of pulling her back into his arms, he pressed a kiss on the palm of her hand, the inside of her wrist and elbow, her shoulder. He pressed tiny kisses up the side of her neck before taking her lips again and filling his hands with her breasts. He circled his thumbs around her nipples until she moaned and clutched at him for support. Then he quickly removed her jeans and panties and lay with her on the bed.

He caressed her again and again, as if he couldn't get enough. He caressed the hollow of her throat, the curve of her shoulder, the valley between her breasts. He caressed her rosy nipples, the flat smoothness of her stomach, then finally the silky nest of curls between her legs. When he'd found her slick heat, he caressed her until she shivered and clutched at him, until her eyes widened in joyous pleasure and she cried out his name.

Only then did he shed his jeans, removing a foil packet from his back pocket.

"That sure of yourself," she murmured breathlessly.

"Where you're concerned?" His voice was hoarse with passion. "No. Just hopeful. Eternally hopeful." He hurriedly rolled on the protection, then returned to her waiting arms. "I've been ready for this since the day we met," he said against her throat. "Are you ready?"

She nodded and braced herself for the sharp pain she expected. What she didn't expect were the shivers of pleasure that followed. She opened her eyes and saw Gregory's face above her, his eyes closed, his jaw tight, as he fought a battle of self-control. Finally, he opened his eyes and smiled at her as he began to move against her. She knew that for as long as she lived, she'd never be able to forget his face—strong and tender, his eyes hazy with desire.

He slid a hand between their bodies and stroked her until she cried out again. She felt as though she were coming apart and the only thing keeping her together was his arms around her.

Later she lay with her head on his chest as he cuddled her close, his hands caressing her. He pressed little kisses to the top of her head, and she smiled as she tunneled her fingers through the soft curls on his chest and nuzzled his neck. Gradually their caresses became more serious as the passion flared again, but Annabelle winced when he touched her. "Oh Gregory, I don't know if I can so soon."

He smiled tenderly and kissed her. "That's okay,

babe. There are other ways to make love," he said and
slowly began to move down her body, his lips—

"What?" Annabelle sat up in bed, her heart
pounding, her body slick with perspiration. Her
gaze met the inscrutable glowing eyes of the cat,
who'd apparently just jumped onto the bed, jos-
tling her awake.

She sighed and hugged her knees. Some dream,
she thought. Her breasts felt swollen, aching to be
touched. The rest of her felt warm and slick and
ready—and frustrated as hell. She sighed again and
flopped back onto her pillow, staring up at the
ceiling. After about five minutes of this unproduc-
tive activity, she sat back up, turned on her light
and searched through her nightstand for a book,
all the while wondering why her traitorous body
couldn't listen to her infinitely more sensible head.
For once.

Gregory flopped over on his stomach, though
he was careful not to land on the erection that he'd
awakened with after an especially sexy dream. He
pulled his pillow over his head, but that didn't shut
out the memories—or shut off his brain.

He'd dreamed about the first time he'd made
love with Annabelle. She'd been shy and self-con-
scious and so sweetly passionate that he'd nearly
lost his mind. He'd known it was her first time and
he'd been determined to take it slow for her. His
efforts had been hampered by a desire that had

grown to nearly painful proportions in the past three months he'd known her, a desire fed by his equally intense love.

Though he hadn't said anything, it had been a first for him as well—the first time he'd ever made love with someone he was really in love with. The experience had been shattering in its intensity, and as he'd lain awake long after she'd fallen asleep in his arms, he'd allowed himself to dream and to plan.

First they'd move in together. After he graduated and secured a job—maybe with Greenpeace or the Save the Bay Foundation—they'd get married. It would be tough financially for a while, at least until Annabelle had finished college, too, but they'd make it. They'd make it because their love would last forever. They would last forever.

They'd only lasted four more months.

Gregory peered out from beneath his pillow at the lighted dial of his clock. It was a quarter past three, only ten minutes since he'd last checked. He grunted and sat up, running his hand through his hair, then swung his feet out of bed. He'd never been one to sit idly, especially when his brain was wide-awake. And right now his brain seemed intent on torturing him with thoughts of Annabelle. Death by Annabelle, he thought wryly.

He tugged on a T-shirt, shorts, and tennis shoes, intending to try jogging. When he began his jog, he didn't intentionally head in Annabelle's direction, but suddenly found himself more than halfway there. He gave a mental shrug. Since he'd already come this far, he might as well go the rest of the way.

It would be interesting to see if all the lights were out as Virgie and Annabelle slumbered peacefully or if somewhere, in some window, a light burned that would indicate Annabelle wasn't sleeping any better than he. And, with a distinct lack of Christian charity, he hoped it was the latter.

Charity was important, but fair was fair. If he couldn't sleep, neither should she.

She *was* awake. Gregory stood on the street outside Virgie's hundred-year-old farmhouse and looked at the lighted window, the lacy curtains filtering the soft glow into floral patterns on the lawn. Shoving his hands into his pockets, he stared up at the light. He knew it wasn't Virgie's bedroom. It had to be Annabelle.

Maybe she'd simply fallen asleep reading. She used to do that, usually over some textbook she'd been studying. He would save her place, lay the book aside, and slide off her shoes before tucking her into his bed. Often she'd awaken then and they'd put the time to better use than studying. It was a wonder neither of them had flunked a single subject that year. He'd certainly done less studying once he'd met her. He'd been more intrigued with Annabelle—intrigued with the passion between them, but also with her ideas and opinions.

He wondered what she was doing now. Maybe she'd only gotten up to get a drink of water. He pictured her stumbling downstairs to the kitchen, hair tousled, eyes at half-mast. She had always been so cute when she'd awakened from a dead sleep—as soft and cuddly and boneless as a drowsy kitten. She'd also been a danger to herself, always walking into doors or stubbing her toes. He'd loved playing knight to his sleepy-eyed lady, leading her in the right direction while she mumbled that her eyes didn't function when she first woke up.

She used to sleep in his T-shirts—on the rare occasions she wore anything at all. Did she still sleep in the nude? His body quickened again at the thought. Maybe she wore lacy nightgowns. No, she wasn't the type. She was more the silky pajamas or the cotton nightshirt type.

It was silly to stand down here on the street and wonder. Chances were, she'd fallen asleep on her bed still dressed in jeans, with an open book in her hands. He turned to jog back home, then froze as he saw a figure moving in her room. Yes, she was awake, after all.

She moved closer to the window, and Gregory withdrew into the shadows as she pulled back the lace curtains and opened the window higher. She leaned out, bracing her hands on the sill.

Gregory drew in his breath. Well, that was one question answered. It wasn't satin pajamas or a cotton nightshirt that she slept in. His gaze caressed the spaghetti straps and minuscule bodice of the slinky nightgown that skimmed over the generous curves of her breasts. He rubbed his hand over the back of his neck. This was certainly enough to keep him awake for the rest of the night.

She turned to look in his direction, and even though he was fairly certain she couldn't see him, he backed up, right into the waiting embrace of the holly bush that provided the church with a bountiful supply of decorative branches every Christmas. He gritted his teeth as the prickly leaves scratched him, and moved forward a few inches. That movement was enough to catch Annabelle's eye.

She leaned farther out the window, and a sliver of moonlight caught the pale skin of her bare shoulders and danced off the soft curls of her hair. Moonlight loved Annabelle, turning her skin to silver and shimmering in her hair like stardust. Of course, sunlight loved Annabelle, too, kissing her creamy skin with gold and sparkling from her eyes.

"Who's there?" she called.

Gregory stiffened his back and stepped out where she could see him. "Just me, Annabelle."

"Gregory? What are you doing skulking around in the shrubbery?"

"I'm not skulking," he said defensively. "I was out jogging and noticed your light was on, that's all."

"Do you always jog into holly bushes?"

Threads of amusement ran through her voice. "And after three in the morning, no less?"

He walked to just under her window as she leaned on her forearms and looked down at him. For a breathless moment he watched as her breasts strained against the low-cut top of her gown. He ignored her question and asked one of his own. "Can't sleep either?"

She shrugged, and he swallowed hard as one silky strap slid off her shoulder. "I was reading."

"You're reading at this hour?"

"You're jogging at this hour?"

"Touché." He looked up at her for a moment, then said impulsively, "Come down and walk with me."

She hesitated for so long, he figured she was going to say no, but she said, "I'll be right down." Five minutes later she stepped out the front door, dressed in shorts and a T-shirt.

"So, let's walk," she said, and headed down the street at a brisk pace.

Gregory hastened to catch up and they walked in companionable silence for several minutes. "Why couldn't you sleep?" he finally asked.

"Why couldn't you?" she countered.

"I don't know. I had things on my mind, I guess."

She sent him an oblique look. "Yeah. Me too."

SIX

As they walked along, Gregory thought several times that he might ask Annabelle what he so desperately wanted to know, but the night was beautiful and the silence between them companionable. He didn't want to spoil it. The warm night air was heady with the scent of honeysuckle and stars sparkled in the black velvet of the sky. It seemed as if they were the only two people in the world.

He reached out and took her hand, and although she looked at him in surprise, she didn't pull away. They walked past the Food Mart, the hardware store, the dry cleaners.

They walked as far as the new shopping center, which was White Creek's main concession to the 1990s. The center consisted of a tiny video store that was part of the equally tiny drugstore, Caterina Jones's children's-wear shop, Muriel Parker's

Beauty Salon, Manny Parker's Barbershop, and Dr. Bill Parker's Pain-free Dentistry.

"I see the Parkers are the leading entrepreneurs in White Creek," Annabelle murmured.

"Next to the Wilsons, I guess."

"Don't Muriel and Manny also have a daughter? I wonder what she's up to these days."

"Trying to get a husband," Gregory muttered.

Annabelle grinned in comprehension. "Trying to get a preacher husband, no doubt."

"No doubt." Gregory's voice was so dry that Annabelle laughed outright.

"Your fault, you know," she said. "You should have taken ugly classes before becoming a minister. It's such a respectable occupation and all. I would imagine that ministers rank right up there on the desirable husband list."

"Right behind doctors and lawyers," he said.

"And dentists?" Annabelle gestured at Bill Parker's sign.

"And dentists. He hadn't been out of dental college for a month before he got snatched up by Maud Greeley's daughter."

"So how have you managed to escape unscathed? Your single status must grate on the nerves of every self-respecting mother and grandmother in the whole town."

"I guess I just evade faster than they can matchmake," he said lightly. "But they do seem to make marrying me off one of their civic duties, along with soliciting donations for the volunteer fire department."

They walked silently for a few more minutes, then Annabelle said, "You know, it's funny, but I've missed it here. I've missed Lute Simpson and Magda, Bosco Wilson's Food Mart, even Clara Walling and her silly Brahma bull. And I've missed Danni. She and I used to be so close, not only cousins, but best friends. We've talked on the phone a lot and she's come to Raleigh on occasion, but somehow it's not the same."

"Then why haven't you been back to visit more often? I know Virgie has missed you a great deal."

Annabelle pulled her hand from his and kept walking. "I call her every week and I always saw her when she came to Raleigh," she said defensively. "She's always come at least twice a year to visit Mother and Dad."

"I'm not accusing you of neglecting your grandmother, Annabelle. I know you talked to her a lot and sent her little gifts now and then, but if you missed White Creek so much, then why didn't you come back to visit more?" He fell silent a moment, then added, "I've sometimes thought that you didn't come back because of me."

"I came back for Danni and Sebastian's wedding."

"Five years ago. And you only stayed a week."

"I've been busy."

"Right."

"Besides, I'm here now."

He reached out and captured her hand again. "Yes, you are. And I'm glad you're back." He was afraid the words rang too true and hastened to add, "The town really needs someone like you here, someone who's so good with children. We have so few activities for kids. I do what I can at the church, but I don't always have the time and I know I don't have the kind of imagination to think up creative and challenging ideas to keep kids interested."

He pulled her to a stop. "Since you're thinking about living here now that you're going to be working in Norfolk, maybe you wouldn't mind taking on a Sunday-school class. We really need one for the ten-to-thirteen-year-olds."

"I hardly think I'm the Sunday-school-teacher type," she protested.

"And what is the Sunday-school-teacher type?"

"You know. Sweet and nice and old-fashioned."

"And no one in their right mind would ever call you sweet or nice," he teased. "C'mon, Annabelle. Danni has a Sunday-school class and she's certainly not a Sunday-school-teacher type—not unless Sunday-school teachers wear pink and purple all the time and have husbands who talk to animals. There are no stereotypical Sunday-school teachers. At least not here. And, after all, I'm not exactly your stereotypical preacher type."

She smiled a little. "I guess you're not, at that. How many preachers get arrested as animal-rights activists or"—she gestured at his hair—"wear the flames of hell on their heads?"

Gregory grinned. "Or get benched during a church baseball game for yelling at the umpire. Just think about it, Annabelle. Or if you'd rather not teach Sunday school, maybe you wouldn't mind being youth activity coordinator."

Annabelle considered that. Youth activity coordinator. The idea appealed to her, but she wouldn't do it unless she knew she could handle being around Gregory without her emotions becoming further entangled. "I'll think about it," was all she said.

They walked a little ways farther to the banks of Denning's Creek, where the clear water bubbled and frothed over a bed of stones. Annabelle leaned back against Taylor's Rock, one of the large granite boulders that flanked the creek on either side just before it widened at Willard's Pasture. Gregory climbed on top of the rock and sat, legs drawn up.

"Did you ever used to swim here?" he asked.

"Danni and I used to, but it was up farther, just past Willard's. It's wider there and deeper. That was the local skinny-dipping hole."

"Skinny-dipping? I can't picture you skinny-dipping." The thoughtful tone in his voice, however, told Annabelle that was exactly what he was doing.

"I was a kid, what can I say? Surely you did your share. I remember you telling me about the pond on your parents' property. Didn't you and your siblings ever take advantage of it?"

"Oh, maybe once or twice," he said, and she could hear the laughter in his voice.

"More than once or twice, I bet. You probably—" She broke off with a squeal.

"What's wrong?"

"There's something moving on the ground near my foot. I think it's a snake," she said, her voice low and tight. "A big one."

Gregory grasped her beneath her arms and hoisted her up onto the rock, then peered closely at the ground, well illuminated by the nearly full moon. Suddenly he let out a hoot of laughter and slid down from the rock. He held up a gecko that couldn't have been longer than six or seven inches. "Here's your python." The little lizard wiggled until he set it back down and it scurried off.

Annabelle shrugged. "Looked like a snake to me. And it's closely enough related that I don't care if it has legs or not. Had I been Eve in the Garden of Eden, we'd still be there, because I never would have gotten close enough to the serpent to take a bite of that apple."

Gregory looked up at her, her hair soft and tousled, glowing with silver streaks of moonlight, her features shadowed and mysterious. He was hit with another stab of the desire that had awakened him earlier.

He remembered his first date with Annabelle— not counting the shared hot dog at the rally. They had gone to a movie, then for a walk. It had been a brisk, chilly night in early October, and Annabelle had sworn she'd seen a snake. Even though Gregory had assured her there wouldn't have been any snakes out at that time of year, she'd still clung to his arm. He'd already been turned on by sitting next to her in the dark theater, their jeans-clad legs touching, her hair—longer then—brushing his arm, their fingers entwined.

He'd felt her breast press against him. It hadn't mattered that she wore a sweater and he a jacket, he'd felt it as strongly as if it had been bare skin on bare skin. He'd looked down at her and she'd turned her face up to his. In the streetlight, her cheeks had been flushed pink with cold, her eyes sparkling, her lips parted. Gregory had known he wouldn't last another minute without kissing her.

As much as he'd wanted to kiss her then, he wanted to kiss her more now. In the moonlight, she looked almost the same as she had nine years ago, and what he couldn't see well, he had no trouble imagining. Her cheeks would still be pink, though from laughter, not cold, her eyes sparkling with merriment. A man would have to be made of stone not to kiss her now. And Gregory certainly wasn't made of stone. At least not all of him, he thought as he noticed the increasingly snug fit of his shorts.

He climbed back up on the rock and sat, legs outstretched, and tried to tell himself that kissing her was a bad idea. He could think of lots of reasons not to kiss her. Weren't things confused enough? Did they really know each other anymore? Wasn't it better to let sleeping dogs lie? Would kissing her really change anything? Would she still run away afterward, leaving him more bewildered than before?

He could think of only one reason to kiss her. It was inevitable. And he'd never been one to fight the inevitable. Still, that was assuming she'd allow him to kiss her. He turned to her and touched her face, angling it so it caught the glow from the moon. Still, he couldn't read anything from her expression.

"What are you looking at me like that for?"

She might have meant her words to sound belligerent, he thought, but to him they merely sounded breathless. "For a minute there," he said softly, "you looked like you did on our first date."

"The rally?"

"No, the movie. It was that Italian movie that won an Oscar for best foreign-language film and we went for a walk afterward."

Annabelle remembered. They'd shared their first kiss that night. They'd been standing under a streetlight while Gregory had tried to convince her that snakes weren't active in cold weather. Only she hadn't thought it was cold. She'd looked at him and felt warm all over. He'd touched her and her blood had grown hotter still. She'd leaned back against the lamppost and looked up at him, silently wishing he'd kiss her. And he had, with lips that were firm, moist, seeking.

She contrasted that with the kiss she'd received after the rehearsal on Tuesday night. Gregory's lips had again been firm, moist, and seeking. They had also been knowledgeable, infinitely more experienced, and demanding. Heaven help her, she wanted to feel those lips now. She knew it was crazy, she knew it could only make a complicated situation worse. She didn't care.

His hand still lingered on her cheek, and she looked at him, wondering if he could see the longing on her face. Maybe he did, because he slid his hand around the back of her neck and gently urged her closer. She balanced herself with her hands as she leaned forward. When their faces were only a few inches apart, Gregory paused and his gaze searched hers.

He always seemed to have a question in his eyes, she thought, and one day she'd ask him what answer it was he kept searching for. But not now. Now she wanted him to kiss her. He did.

Their lips touched, tentatively at first, lightly, tenderly. But they grew hungrier, wanting to taste, to savor, to devour. His tongue slid over and around hers, and hers returned the intimate caress. His hand wove through her hair and tugged her nearer, and she lost her balance and fell against him.

Her breasts nestled against his chest as if they'd come home, her legs straddled his hard-muscled thigh. She knew he could feel her feminine heat by the way he shifted, enabling her to settle more fully against him. She looked at him, and the soft silver moonlight revealed his face—his nostrils flaring as if he were a male animal scenting his mate, his lips parting, ready to taste, his features tight with wanting.

He smoothed her hair back from her face, then cradled her head in his hands and urged her mouth to his. He took possession surely, thoroughly, his tongue advancing, then retreating, encouraging hers to follow. Somehow she knew that he didn't just want to kiss her, he wanted her to kiss him. Accepting his kisses wasn't good enough, he wanted her to actively seek them.

He smoothed his hands over her shoulders, down her arms and up again, then he lay back on the boulder, pulling her down with him. She sprawled on him, her softness seeking and finding the corresponding hard planes of his body. As she pressed her hands flat on his chest, she could feel his heart beating.

Strands of her hair fell forward, providing a silken curtain of privacy around them as he kissed her again and again. She felt his hands slide beneath the edge of her T-shirt and caress the hot skin of her back, then slip beneath the elastic waist of her shorts and tease the edge of her silky panties.

She wanted to touch him, too, to see if his flesh was as hot as hers felt, so she levered up a little and tugged up the front of his T-shirt. He groaned as she glided her hands over his chest, tunneling her fingers through the silky golden-brown hair that dusted it before searching for and finding his small erect nipples.

He gasped with pleasure and moved his hands beneath her shirt again, to explore the bare skin of her back, restlessly, searchingly. Finally, he tugged her shirt up as well, then her bra, without even bothering to unfasten it.

When bare skin met bare skin, they both groaned in satisfaction, and their mouths and tongues met in another passionate duel. Gregory spread his legs and Annabelle's thigh slipped between them, rubbing against his swollen desire.

He rolled her beneath him, his arms keeping her bare back from contact with the cool stone. Lowering his head to her breast, he took a hardened nipple between his teeth and nibbled lightly, before drawing it into his mouth. Annabelle's eyes fluttered closed at the incredible rivers of sensation that were spreading through her veins, and her fingers wove through his hair, holding his tormenting mouth to her. He suckled as if he were empty inside and only her taste could fill him.

He turned his attention to her other breast before moving up to take her lips again. He kidnapped her breath and held it hostage, allowing her to ransom it only by opening her mouth wider to his possession. She arched her hips beneath him and he answered with an instinctive thrust of his own, his erection settling against her softness.

"Oh, Annie, it's been so long," he murmured against her lips.

Nobody had called her Annie in nine years, and the name was like a dousing of cold water. Annabelle struggled to sit up, hastily pulling down her T-shirt and fumbling to get her bra back in place.

"Annie?" Gregory's voice was laced with frustration and confusion.

"I haven't been Annie for a long time now," she said. "For nine years, in fact."

He sat up, drawing in a deep breath and finger-combing his hair into spikes that glinted fire even in the moonlight. "I don't understand."

She wondered if her voice sounded as breathless as his. "I—this isn't a good idea, Rev."

"I see the 'Rev' is back again," he muttered, and hopped off the boulder. He moved rather gingerly in deference to the erection that Annabelle could still see outlined by the front of his shorts.

He held up his hand to her. "Come on down, Annabelle. It's time to go home."

"Gregory—"

"I'm sorry, Annabelle. You're right. This isn't a good idea. It's also not appropriate behavior for a preacher. I have an example to uphold."

"Do you have to be saintly all the time? Don't preachers get to be human on their days off? Aren't you allowed the same feelings as the rest of mankind, or are you only allowed to feel within the sanctity of marriage?"

"I do feel just like everyone else. I think you know how much I feel. And, surprisingly enough, no, I don't think you have to be married."

"You don't believe in marriage?"

"I do believe in marriage. I believe in commitment more. Some people are married without commitment. Some people are committed without marriage. Which one's better? The answer's pretty obvious."

"So you don't have to be married to have sex."

"I think making love should be just that. Making love. Two people in love who are committed to their relationship. No, I don't think you have to be married. You just have to be committed."

"And you're not committed to me."

"Do you want me to be?"

"Well, no. Of course not." Annabelle wanted to wince at how weak and lame her voice sounded.

"So, what's going on, then? You were the one who called a halt a minute ago. Why are you trying to turn it into some kind of issue now?"

She didn't answer. He was right, she *was* trying to make a big issue out of it. Why?

"Besides," he added, "I got the message."

What message? She wanted to ask him. How could he get her message when she didn't even know what it was? Her head felt so jumbled, she couldn't pin down a thought if she tried, and she was damned if she knew what she was saying or doing.

Faint rosy streaks of light were finger-painting the horizon by the time they arrived back at Virgie's. The walk back had been every bit as uncomfortable and silent as the earlier walk had been comfortable and chatty.

"Good night, Annabelle. Thanks for the walk."

"I—you're welcome." Things were so strained, she could have cried. "I'll—I'll see you around, I guess."

"Yeah." Gregory turned and walked off, not pausing to look back even once. Annabelle watched him for a moment, then opened the door and went inside.

Merlin sat in the middle of the living room and began to meow and wrap himself around her ankles as soon as she crossed the threshold. "It's not your breakfast time," she muttered, but he kept meowing. "Look, you're smart enough to do just about anything you want, why don't you learn to tell time?"

She went into the kitchen and fixed him a bowl of Cheerios, not wanting him to wake up her grandmother. She didn't particularly want to explain to Gran that she'd been running around the neighborhood half the night with the minister. Not that her grandmother would be shocked. Annabelle doubted she'd even be mildly surprised. She wasn't sure what it would take to actually shock her grandmother. Maybe if she'd been running around the neighborhood naked with the minister. Boy oh boy, did her mind circle around *that* idea. But she doubted even that would shock Gran. More than likely, she'd be standing on the sidelines cheering.

Yawning, Annabelle went upstairs. She didn't bother changing out of her shorts and T-shirt, just crawled into bed still wearing them and buried her face in the soft feather pillow. Lord, she needed some sleep, she thought. Nice, uninterrupted sleep. She just prayed she wouldn't dream about Gregory this time.

She was awakened by a tap on her bedroom door. "Honey, are you gonna sleep all day?"

"Huh?" Annabelle forced open one eye. "What time is it, Gran?"

"About eleven. Daisy dropped by. She's waiting downstairs. I'll tell her you'll be down in a few minutes."

Annabelle stumbled, literally, to the bathroom. After a quick shower, she felt a little more human, so she took the time to camouflage the signs of her lack of sleep with some concealer beneath her eyes. Smiling brightly, she went downstairs.

Though Daisy looked like her sisters, there was something different about her. Even when they were kids and the triplets used to delight in fooling people, Annabelle and Danni had always been able to tell them apart. Rose was gentler, more subdued; Lily was a fighter, standing up for her rights —for anyone's rights, for that matter.

And Daisy? Daisy had always been more flamboyant, as vibrant as a flame. And about as constant. Annabelle wasn't surprised that this was her third engagement this year. What would surprise her would be if Daisy actually went through with the wedding.

Daisy stood when Annabelle entered the room and gave her a quick hug. "I had a few minutes to spare and thought I'd drop by. We haven't had much time to catch up since your return to the wilds of Virginia."

"I dropped by your house yesterday and nobody was there."

"I had the day off and went into Norfolk with Mother to check with the florist."

"It's hard to believe you're getting married."

Daisy fidgeted with a lock of the light brown hair she'd added a few blond streaks to. "I'm the same age as you. That's plenty old enough to be married."

"I mean, I just didn't picture you settling down so soon."

"And I always pictured you being married long before now. You always liked kids, even when you were just a kid yourself."

"Yeah, well, things don't always turn out the way you expect them to, do they?"

"True enough." Daisy stretched out her tanned legs, crossing one over the other. A half-dozen ankle bracelets tinkled as she moved. "All of us expected you to graduate college and get married to that guy you were so gung-ho over."

Annabelle stifled a sigh. Daisy knew darn well it was Gregory she'd been so gung-ho over, but this was her idea of being subtle. "So instead I graduated college and went for my master's degree. And I'm glad I did. I love teaching."

"Don't you ever wonder what might have happened if you'd married, though?"

"No! Not at all. Everything turned out for the best."

"I wonder if Gregory thinks so."

"Tell me more about your wedding. I love the bridesmaid's dress. What's your dress like? Do you know where you're going on your honeymoon?"

Annabelle managed to sidetrack Daisy, no easy task, into talking about her upcoming nuptials. At least Annabelle assumed they'd be upcoming, though with Daisy you could never be sure. For someone who was supposed to be in love, Daisy seemed awfully offhand about the whole thing.

They talked for another hour or so before Daisy glanced at her watch, bounced up, and dashed out the door, late for her afternoon date with Buddy. Annabelle couldn't help but think that she'd never been late for a date with Gregory. As a matter of fact, she'd usually been early, as eager as he for their evenings together. Once they'd moved in together, they'd stopped going out at all, except to classes or his infernal demonstrations and rallies.

It had seemed silly to go to the movies when they ended up necking and missing the whole thing. It was equally silly to go out for pizza when they could have it delivered and never have to get out of bed, except to answer the door. Annabelle could remember the sight of Gregory's cute bare buns as he reached around the door, trying to juggle the pizza and the money in one hand while making sure the door stayed between him and the delivery boy.

Even though Annabelle had told Daisy she'd never wondered what would have happened if she'd married Gregory, she had. Often. When she had been with Gregory, she figured that by the time she was the age she was now, she'd have been married at least eight years and she and Gregory would be thinking about starting a family—if they hadn't already.

As she looked back she had to wonder how their marriage would have survived if Gregory had really gotten his dream job—aboard the Greenpeace ship, *The Rainbow Warrior*, or aboard a ship working for the Save the Bay Foundation. How long would he have been gone at a time? Days? Weeks? Months? Could their marriage have stood such separations? Knowing how much she'd resented the afternoons and evenings he'd donated to his causes, wouldn't she have ended up hating his job even more?

The problem was that if she had just met Gregory this summer, she would have found him enormously attractive. Charming, even. She would have definitely wanted to get to know him better, especially since she wouldn't know his history of putting his causes first. But she hadn't just met him and she knew all about his history. She'd been part of it.

SEVEN

Rehearsal for the Fourth of July pageant went off without a hitch that night. The kids had all learned their lines and were ready to present their program on Sunday night. Annabelle didn't see Gregory, though, and wasn't sure whether she was relieved or disappointed by his absence.

As they were finishing up she heard piano music trickling down the stairs. It was sweet and up-tempo and she could hear the muffled sound of voices singing in harmony. George Washington—she kept forgetting whether he was Jordan or Ethan Wainscott—said it was choir practice, moved from Wednesday to Thursday night so the piano could be tuned Thursday morning.

When she'd seen the last kid out the door and watched the Wainscott boys run across the street to their white frame house, she went upstairs to take a peek.

She recognized a lot of the people—Lute Simpson, Caterina Jones, Clara Walling, Muriel and Manny Parker. There were fourteen people total, not counting the broad shouldered pianist. With a start, she realized she recognized those shoulders. It was Gregory.

She hugged the doorway as she watched him move his fingers over the yellowed ivory keys of the rather battered upright piano that she recognized from when she was a child. It still wore the same decals of Old Testament figures they'd studied during Vacation Bible School—Daniel in the lions' den, David and Goliath, Joseph and his coat of many colors. Seeing Gregory sitting at the same piano was a strange and disconcerting blending of her childhood, her recent past, and the present.

Annabelle shook her head. This was just too, too weird. She hadn't even known Gregory could play the piano, and play it so well, at that. Had he learned since college or had he always known and never shared it with her?

She hadn't told him every last little thing about herself, but somehow she'd felt she'd known everything there was to know about him. Maybe it was arrogant of her, but it was unsettling to think there were things she'd hadn't known after all. She wondered what other secrets he hadn't shared with her.

He stopped playing and Lute made a comment that had Gregory throwing back his head in laughter. Annabelle's stomach tightened. There was that laugh again—full-bodied, nothing held back, inviting the world to join in. She found it as compelling as she always had. A woman could listen to a laugh like that for the rest of her life.

Not liking that train of thought, Annabelle took a step back, intending to leave silently and unseen. At that moment one of the Wainscott boys dashed up the stairs and into the room. He whispered something to Gregory and Annabelle saw an expression of shock mingled with pain cross Gregory's face. He said something to the choir and turned to leave.

He almost walked by Annabelle without seeing her, then stopped. "Annabelle. What are you doing here?"

Without thinking, she laid her hand on his arm. "What's wrong?"

"Hilary Cochran just had a heart attack and they've taken her to Norfolk."

"I remember Mrs. Cochran. She was my Sunday-school teacher for a lot of the summers I spent here. I liked her a lot. I guess you're going to the hospital?" Silly question, Annabelle thought, but Gregory used to have a near phobia about hospitals.

He blamed it on a blackout that occurred when he was in the hospital for a tonsillectomy. He'd been visiting his grandparents at the time and the hospital in the small town where they lived had a generator that only provided enough energy for the intensive-care unit and surgery floors. Just four years old, he'd been in a strange and scary place for hours in the dark.

He nodded. "This time I'll be there not only as her minister but as a friend. She's been the closest thing to family I have here."

Annabelle saw so many emotions mingling on his face. Worry, shock, even a little fear. And the pain of a man who didn't want to lose a dear friend. "I'd like to go with you." She wasn't sure what made her say it, but was glad she'd offered when she saw him relax a little in relief.

"If you want to. I'd appreciate the company."

She walked with him out to the parking lot. "Shall I drive?"

"Would you mind?"

"Of course not. Yours or mine?"

"Yours will be all right."

She slipped behind the wheel of her car and unlocked the door for Gregory. "I see you remembered to lock your doors for a change," he said with a ghost of a smile.

"Tell me how you and Mrs. Cochran got to be so close."

He gazed out the window, then said quietly, "When I first came to town, I felt very alone. I'd just been ousted from my church—that kind of rejection stays with a man for a while—and I didn't know a soul in town. Hilary's daughter had just remarried and moved up to Arlington and Hilary was feeling a little lonely too. And bored. She'd retired at sixty from some office supply company over in Waverly and was at loose ends."

He smiled slightly. "She decided to occupy her time by decorating the children's Sunday-school rooms. She hand-stenciled rabbits and ducks all over the nursery walls and painted a huge ark with all kinds of animals in the preschool classroom. I'm not saying she's the world's best artist, mind you, but there's a lot of love and joy in everything she's painted."

"She always took Danni and me under her wings when we spent summers here. She'd come by Gran's whenever we got here and catch us up on what the Sunday-school class was learning so we'd never feel left out. When we were too old for her classes, she used to volunteer us to help out with Vacation Bible School. It made Danni and me feel so important." Annabelle sighed. "She was always willing to work with kids."

"She always reminded me of you that way."

Annabelle cast a quick glance at Gregory. "Me?"

"Sure. Don't you think I noticed? Every time there was anything going on that had to do with children, you were always right in the thick of things."

She shrugged. "That was just because I was the head of my sorority's special project committee and we always seemed to pick projects that had something to do with kids."

"Maybe, but you volunteered to head that

committee and you were the one who seemed to propose those projects."

Annabelle didn't answer. That was one of the things she'd never really mentioned to Gregory, yet he'd noticed it anyway. Odd, a little voice whispered in the back of her mind, that she'd had her causes too.

They were silent most of the rest of the drive to Norfolk. When they reached the hospital, Annabelle dropped Gregory off at the door. "I'll go park the car while you find out what floor Mrs. Cochran is on. I'll catch up."

Gregory waited for Annabelle in the lobby, and after she'd made a quick call to her grandmother to let her know where she was, they caught the elevator up to the cardiac intensive-care unit. Annabelle watched as Gregory talked briefly to the doctor, then sat next to Hilary Cochran's best friend, Ada Wilson, Bosco's mother. He took her thin wrinkled hands in his and spoke so softly that Annabelle couldn't hear, but it wasn't long before Ada smiled a little and her taut shoulders relaxed.

Gregory was allowed to see Mrs. Cochran for a few minutes, and when he came out, he had a smile for Ada. Only Annabelle noticed the shadows in his eyes and the lines that seemed more deeply etched in his forehead. When he came over to sit next to her, she said nothing, just took his hand and gave it a companionable squeeze.

Mrs. Cochran's daughter, Pat, and her husband arrived about midnight, apparently having driven down from Arlington at breakneck speed. They were allowed into CICU for a few minutes, and when they came out, Pat burst into tears. Gregory sat and talked with her while her husband went to make some phone calls.

It was a long night, and Annabelle marveled at how Gregory managed to be unfailingly gentle, supportive, comforting. She also wondered why no one seemed to notice that this was taking such a toll on him. The shadows in his eyes were increasingly dark, his shoulders seemed almost bowed by the weight he was carrying as he submerged the part of himself that was the worried friend and carried on as the caring minister.

Toward dawn, when Pat and her husband, Tim, had dozed off in their chairs and Bosco had come to insist Ada go home, Annabelle went to get a cup of coffee for Gregory. She came back to find him slumped in his chair, his head in his hands. She sat beside him and set the coffee down, then, without thinking, ran a comforting hand over his head. Wordlessly, he turned to her and pulled her into his arms, burying his face in her neck. He held her tightly, as if trying to absorb her. She clung just as tightly, willing to let him draw whatever he needed from her.

The doctor came by about six and Gregory stood with Pat and Tim as they talked with him, then he came back over to Annabelle.

"How is she?" Annabelle asked softly.

"Holding her own. The doctor says the next few hours will tell."

"Are you okay?"

Gregory looked at her strangely and waited a long moment before answering. "Funny," he finally said, "I don't think I ever remember anyone asking me that in this kind of situation."

"They should have. Anyone can see you're as worried and concerned as everyone else is. So, are you okay?"

He ran the tips of his fingers down her cheek. "I'm okay. But I'm glad you're here."

"Why don't you sit down and catch a catnap? I'll wake you if anyone needs you."

He shook his head and took a sip of the now lukewarm coffee. "I'm fine. I've done with less sleep than this."

Annabelle reached out and took the cup from him, setting it aside. "I'm sure you have, but it's not necessary right now for you to turn yourself into a zombie from lack of sleep. Relax, close your eyes. I'll wake you if you're needed for anything. I promise."

A tiny smile played about his lips as he looked at her. "You're going to hound me until I do what you say, aren't you?"

"Darn right I am!"

"What a bossy little thing you've turned out to be," he murmured as he sat back in his chair and leaned his head against the wall. He looked at her again, letting his gaze wander over her features one by one, before his eyelids drifted closed.

Annabelle sat next to him, watching until his muscles relaxed and his breathing slowed in sleep. Pat and her husband went downstairs to the cafeteria for breakfast after Annabelle promised to come get them if there was any change.

Alone, Annabelle yawned and rubbed her burning eyes. She'd had less than her usual eight hours sleep the night before last and none at all this past night. She massaged her temples, trying to forestall the beginnings of a headache. She was getting too old to handle sleepless nights, she thought.

In college it hadn't been as much of a problem. She could remember lots of nights when she and Gregory would study throughout the evening, then make love until the early morning. Of course, sitting in a whitewalled, antiseptic-scented hospital waiting room all night was a far cry from making passionate love.

No, it wasn't making love. Annabelle thought of how Gregory had comforted Pat, how he'd prayed by Mrs. Cochran's bedside, how he'd stayed all night in a hospital when he still hated them. No, certainly not making love, but an act of love, nonetheless.

He *loved* these people. He loved them with a pure and unselfish love. He wasn't just mouthing comforting platitudes. He meant them. Suddenly Annabelle wanted to touch him. Simply touch him.

Impulsively, she reached out and laid her hand on his arm.

He opened his eyes, blinked a couple of times, then looked at her. "Is everything all right?"

She'd forgotten what a light sleeper he was. Color flooded her face. "I didn't mean to wake you. I'm sorry. Everything's fine. I just—just—" She fell silent. *I just wanted to touch you? I just needed to reassure myself that you weren't too good to be true?*

He didn't press her to finish her sentence. Laying his hand over hers, he leaned his head back against the wall. "What time is it?"

"Probably between seven-thirty and eight. They've been rolling carts of breakfast trays up and down the hall."

He grinned at the sound of distaste in her voice. "Still not a morning person, are you? You always said it was a crime against nature to eat before ten."

"If it isn't, it ought to be."

"Maybe you should bring that up at the next town council meeting. Especially if you're planning to stay in White Creek."

Annabelle shrugged, not yet willing to commit herself one way or the other. First she had to determine whether she could get her rapidly escalating feelings about Gregory back under strict control.

"Where are Pat and Tim?" he asked.

"Downstairs eating breakfast. I promised you'd

come get them if they were needed. Can I bring you some more coffee or something to eat? I think they have sausage biscuits or some such."

"I'm okay for now. But you get something if you want."

"At this hour?"

He smiled. "Sorry, I forgot myself."

A nurse came out of the CICU and walked over to Gregory. "Excuse me. Are you Mrs. Cochran's son?"

"No, I'm her minister."

"Then she'd like to see you for a few minutes. No more than five." The nurse's expression plainly said that she wished Gregory were her minister, though Annabelle doubted she wanted his guidance on spiritual matters.

Gregory turned to Annabelle. "I'll be right back."

"That's okay," she said, still looking sourly at the nurse. She was hit with a sudden urge to print OFF LIMITS in big letters across Gregory's shirt. Annabelle caught her breath, surprised she felt that way. Then terrified. She folded her arms across her chest and huddled back down in her chair, glad Gregory was with Mrs. Cochran for a few minutes. She needed to pull herself together.

This wasn't supposed to happen, she told herself, and wondered if there was a hospital someplace where she could get an injection of common sense or a brain transplant. Or, she thought hopefully, maybe just a good night's sleep.

———◆———◆———

About nine o'clock Mrs. Cochran's son, Richard, and his wife, Susan, arrived from Ohio. Annabelle remembered Richard, who was a few years older than she, from her summers in White Creek. Richard had been a dark-haired, dark-eyed teenager who'd had most of the girls between fifteen and twenty-five at his heels. Still, he'd always been pleasant, even to Virgie Pace's gawky and curious grandchildren.

Annabelle slipped down to the cafeteria to call her grandmother, then got cups of hot coffee to carry upstairs. She handed out the coffee, then sat down out of the way and watched Gregory and the others. Suddenly she couldn't see Gregory, the boy, at all. There was only Gregory, the man. Gregory, the minister.

She leaned her head against the wall and wondered tiredly where the boy had gone all of a sudden. Even two nights ago, as they'd walked in the moonlight, she'd seen glimpses of the boy she'd loved so long ago, through the new and improved Gregory. This morning, the boy was nowhere to be found. She closed her aching eyes for a moment, wondering if she still carried traces of the girl she used to be or if they had disappeared just as suddenly.

"Annabelle?"

"Mm?"

"Annabelle."

Her eyelids fluttered, then opened. "Gregory?" She realized immediately where she was and hastened to sit up straight, smoothing a hand over her hair. "Sorry, I must have dozed off a minute."

"More like a couple of hours, but that's all right. You were tired."

"So are you."

He shrugged. "Comes with the territory."

"How's Mrs. Cochran?"

"The doctor was by a few minutes ago and it looks like she's come through the worst of it. Her family is with her now. I thought I'd go and get a few things done, then come back later today." He held out his hand. "C'mon. Let's go home."

Without even thinking twice, she put her hand in his. He curled his fingers around it and tugged her to her feet, but didn't release her hand as they went downstairs and walked out to the parking lot. Annabelle blinked at the brightness of the morning sun and stumbled a little.

"You okay?"

She nodded. "I seem to have forgotten how obnoxiously bright July sunshine can be."

Gregory stifled a yawn. "I've noticed the same thing. And doesn't it always seem that the more tired you are, the brighter it gets?"

She unlocked the passenger door for him, and he took her other hand in his too. "Thanks for coming with me, Annabelle. It helped to have you there."

"You still don't like hospitals much."

He shook his head. "I doubt I ever will, but I tolerate them because it's necessary. People need somebody with them during times like this."

And what about you, Gregory? she asked silently. *Who's there for you?*

Annabelle pushed a Moody Blues tape into the cassette player and music filled the air. Gregory yawned and rubbed his eyes, itchy from lack of sleep. "Why don't you take a nap as soon as you get home?" she asked.

He sighed. "I'm too tired to sleep."

"So what are you going to do?"

"I had planned to pick out the hymns to go with Sunday's service, but I don't think I'm in any shape to make any decisions right now. I guess I'll mow the church lawn and pick out the hymns tomorrow."

"I thought you usually wrote your sermons on Saturday."

"I'll do that Saturday too. I have the germ of an idea already. The idea you gave me a couple of weeks ago."

"You mean the one about charity being freely given and all that?"

"That's the one." He stifled another yawn.

"I still think you ought to lie down a little while."

"No, I couldn't sleep. Too much adrenaline, I guess."

They fell into a companionable silence, Annabelle softly humming along with "Nights in White Satin," Gregory sneaking glances at her as she watched the road. For the life of him, he couldn't figure her out. Why had she insisted on coming with him last night? Why had she stayed?

She stopped in front of the little house the church provided for its ministers. He turned to thank her for the ride, only to find Annabelle already out her door. Bemused, he got out and followed her as she headed up the sidewalk to his house.

"Well?" she said.

"Well what?" he asked, still trying to figure out what she was up to.

"Well, where's the key?"

"Uh, it's not locked."

She raised her eyebrows. "And all this time you've jumped all over me for not locking my car doors?" She opened the door and went inside, Gregory following behind her.

He stood in his living room, watching her take in the surroundings. He wondered what she thought of the room. It wasn't anything fancy, but it was comfortable, with the overstuffed sofa and chairs and the braided rug on the floor.

He saw her gaze linger on the stack of various environmental journals on the coffee table, then pass on to the Dean Koontz novel lying next to his favorite chair. She finally turned her attention to the eclectic collection of framed posters and pictures on his walls—everything from an expensive and elegant engraving of the Three Wise Men given to him by his father a few years ago, to Greenpeace and PETA posters.

Why was she there? he wondered. "Uh, would you like to sit down?"

"Actually, I'm hungry. I thought I'd fix some toast or something. You do have bread on hand, don't you?"

"Yeah."

"Good. Most single guys I know have just a refrigerator full of six-packs, pretzels, and cookies."

"I don't drink." What single guys? he thought. And how do you know what they have in their refrigerators?

"Right," she said. "What about Communion wine?"

"We use grape juice."

"Oh. Why don't you sit and I'll bring you a couple pieces of toast. Just butter, like you used to like it, and a cup of tea."

Actually he preferred clover honey and coffee now, but he was too tired to argue. He simply sat in the recliner he preferred, and Annabelle reached down and pulled the lever that lifted the footrest.

"Just close your eyes and take it easy. I'll bring the toast when it's done."

Ten minutes later, when Annabelle walked into the room with a plate of buttered toast, Gregory was sound asleep. "I knew if I could just get you to sit for a minute, you'd be out like a light," she whispered, and sat on the arm of the sofa nibbling on a piece of the toast. The lines of fatigue that etched his face had relaxed a little as he slept, and Annabelle felt a peculiar clenching feeling inside as she watched him.

She knew that feeling had some awesome significance to it, but was just too tired to think about it right now. Right now her priority was to make sure Gregory was comfortable, then go home and put herself to bed for a long nap.

She set down the plate of toast and gently tugged off Gregory's sneakers, smiling as she saw the holes in his sweat socks. The boy was back again, she thought, inexplicably glad. Earlier at the hospital, she'd been a little afraid she'd never see him again.

She ran her fingertip lightly about the hole in his left heel. He'd always loved disreputable sneakers and well-worn socks. His socks were always clean, but he'd wear them long past the time when most people would have tossed them out. They were like old friends, he'd said.

Old friends. Old lovers. Only lovers. She still wanted him. Which, all things considered, made about as much sense as wanting an IRS audit. It was just that being in White Creek, which was at the heart of so many of her favorite childhood memories, and seeing Gregory, who was at the heart of her most poignant college memories, was getting things all mixed up.

No, she told herself as she left, *I'm just tired, that's all. Exhausted. I'll take a nap and wake up with a clearer head and all this will fall into place. Into place back in the past where it belongs.*

EIGHT

Gregory woke up when the rays of early-afternoon sun streaming in the windows fell across his face. "Annabelle?" He opened his eyes, but he was alone. Not that he expected her to be there, but it had been a nice thought to wake up with. He glanced at his watch, then got to his feet, noticing the plate of cold toast and tea on the coffee table. He smiled when he saw one nibbled-on piece lying on top of the others.

Which brought him back to his disjointed thinking of earlier that morning. What was with her? Ever since her return to White Creek, she had been making him dizzy with her inconsistency. She pushed him away, pulled him closer, pushed him away again. She acted like she could barely stand to be in the same room with him, then kissed him like there was no tomorrow. She was prickly and wary and always running away—except that she hadn't run away last night. She'd stayed with him, brought him coffee, worried about him. She'd somehow known that he needed her, and she'd been there.

Just a day or two ago he'd wondered what it would be like to have someone there for him. Now he knew. It was almost unbearably sweet and so much easier to be strong when he knew he wasn't alone. Gregory sighed ruefully. At least he hadn't been alone last night. He was alone now, though, with no guarantees about tonight or tomorrow or the next day.

He sighed again and headed for the bathroom, nearly tripping over the cat who sat in the middle of the hall, his yellow-striped tail twitching. "Hello, Merlin." He didn't even wonder how the cat had gotten in.

Over the past five years the cat had come and gone as if he'd owned this house, as well as Danni and Sebastian's and Virgie's. Danni jokingly referred to the cat as Sebastian's familiar. It wouldn't surprise Gregory if that were so. After six years in this odd little town with its vet who could talk to animals, senior citizens who zipped around on motorcycles, and a self-sworn Gypsy, nothing could surprise him.

Except Annabelle. She surprised him in dozens of ways, every time he saw her. She was always lovelier than he remembered—her hair silkier, her eyes softer, her skin creamier. When he reached out to touch her, he never knew whether to expect the sweet fragrance and satiny coolness of rose petals or a handful of thorns. She could be bold or shy, sweet or acerbic, cuddly or prickly. And he seemed to be enchanted with all of her prismatic sides.

When Gregory took his evening stroll—this time at eight P.M. instead of three A.M.—he deliberately headed toward Virgie's house, though he didn't know if Annabelle was there or not. But as if conjured from his thoughts, she sat on the front porch swing. In the rapidly lengthening shadows of twilight, Gregory saw the gleam of her soft hair, the pale gold of her legs, left bare by the short skirt she wore, the creamy skin of her shoulders and arms, exposed by her matching sleeveless top.

Her gaze seemed fixed on the horizon as she stared off into space, and Gregory didn't think she even noticed him as he walked up the sidewalk. He wondered what she was thinking about to put such a wistful, almost pensive expression on her face.

"Annabelle?"

She jumped and turned startled eyes to him, then smiled. "What are you doing here?"

"Taking a walk. I just got back from the hospital a little while ago."

"Oh. How's Mrs. Cochran?"

"Better, I think. Still weak. And, according to Richard, the cardiologist says she's not totally out of the woods yet. But we prayed together and I read her favorite Bible passages to her, and she seemed to enjoy it. I told her you'd stayed the night at the hospital and she'd like you to visit her when she's better."

"I'd like that," Annabelle murmured, then gestured at the other side of the swing. "Wanna sit?"

He didn't hesitate. "Love to."

They sat, swaying back and forth in comfortable silence as the night swallowed up the last of the sun. Fireflies began winking off and on and the night orchestra of peepers tuned up.

He wished he could sit like this with her every summer evening. Knowing she'd be there at the end of each day, waiting to share a few quiet minutes, could make the rest of the day worthwhile. When they'd finished talking about their days with each other, their conversation would turn more intimate and their hands would clasp, fingers entwine. Their world would narrow to exclude everything—the peepers, the fireflies, the warm summer breeze—but the two of them. Finally, they'd get up in unison and go inside, closing the door.

"How long did you sleep today?"

Gregory forced his attention from fantasy to reality. "About three hours, I guess. And you?"

"Not long, maybe an hour. I just can't sleep well during daylight."

"I wanted to thank you."

"For what?"

"For a lot of things." His gaze lingered on her face. "For staying with me last night. It meant more than you can know. And thanks for realizing what I needed. You knew I needed to sleep even when I was denying it."

"You were just like a little kid who says he doesn't need a nap even when he's yawning and his eyelids won't stay open."

"I only hope I wasn't as cranky."

"You were polite and kind. No one could have asked for anyone nicer."

Silence reigned again, and Gregory found himself being seduced by her nearness. He could feel the warmth of her body all along his right side, her arm touching his, her thigh touching his.

Deliberately, he reached over and took her hand, entwining his fingers with hers. Maybe she was as seduced as he by the warm soft darkness because, though she glanced at him, she allowed her hand to rest in his. He closed his eyes for a moment. She was wearing White Shoulders again. He doubted he'd ever be able to smell it without thinking of Annabelle. He could remember breathing in the scent when he'd slide his hands over her skin. The heat of their bodies as they made love seemed to intensify the fragrance until it surrounded them both.

The scent of it now made him long to touch her, but he contented himself with caressing her hand instead. He cradled her hand, his fingers lightly stroking each finger, tracing circles in her palm, gently massaging the fleshy pad between her thumb and forefinger. Barriers momentarily down, her gaze met his and he looked into her unshuttered eyes, knowing she was feeling the same heat he did. It was purer than lust, softer than wanting, warmer than desire.

He bent his head to hers, his lips hovering just out of reach, wanting to give her time to move away. She didn't. He released her hand to brush strands of hair back from her face before moving closer still. Barely a kiss, his lips moved against hers, soft as velvet, slick as satin, seductive as a blazing fire on a cold day. He intended to take one kiss, one taste, then pull away. Until Annabelle opened her mouth to him, until she tunneled her fingers through his hair and urged him closer.

A wave of sweet, heady need surged through him and he kissed her again and again, each kiss a little hungrier, a little more urgent, than the one before. He kissed her until kissing wasn't enough anymore and he closed his hand over her breast. She arched into his touch, the movement making the swing sway. Only then did Gregory remember they were sitting on the front porch, in full view of any interested neighbors.

Annabelle realized it at the same time because she withdrew slightly, running one shaky hand over her hair, smoothing it back behind her ears. She gave him a small smile and shifted to look straight ahead again.

Gregory searched for something to lighten the mood. He didn't want her dwelling on what had just happened, picking it apart, trying to rational-ize her way out of doing it again. A firefly blinked right in front of him, startling them both. Gregory reached out to capture the insect. He opened his hand in front of her and the little beetle crawled across his palm before launching itself back into the air. *"Photuris pennsylvanica."*

Annabelle smiled a little, gratefully accepting the distraction. "Show-off!" She smacked at a mosquito that had dared past the citronella candle on the porch railing. "You think you're so smart, then identify this." She pointed at the persistent pest that was attempting to obtain a snack from the inside of her thigh.

"Mosquito," he said.

"Ha-ha." She absently rubbed the spot where a little red bump was already forming.

"Uh, *Culex pipiens.* I think. Right?"

"How am I supposed to know?"

"Then you wouldn't know if I was right or wrong, would you?"

She smiled and shook her head, her smile suddenly fading when his hand gently moved hers aside and he rubbed his fingertips over the mosquito bite.

He jerked his hand away after a moment and searched for another distraction, this time for his persistently wayward thoughts. A whippoorwill sounded in the distance. "Now that is—"

"Please, don't tell me. There are some things I'd rather not know. I wish I'd never learned that bacon was full of nitrites and I wish I'd never found out that the moon is really a dusty ball of rock. I'm sorry I ever learned that JFK had affairs and I really don't want to know one single botanical fact about whippoorwills."

"Maybe there are some things it's better not to know." Gregory couldn't help but think of the question he'd wanted to ask Annabelle all these years. Did he really want to know the answer? Suddenly he wasn't so sure.

"All I know is whippoorwills sound so lonely," she murmured. "Even when I was a little girl, I always thought so. Gran told Danni and me that they were really singing lullabies for their babies. I know that's not so, but I liked believing it as a child."

Gregory nodded. "I'd like believing that too. You know, I hadn't heard a whippoorwill in years until I moved to White Creek. They don't have too many in downtown Philly where I grew up, or in the heart of the city of Arlington where my first church was."

"I used to hear one on occasion on campus."

"Maybe that's because you took time to stop and listen. I was always running one place or the other."

"Yeah. You were pretty busy. Between your schoolwork and all those demonstrations you were involved in, you hardly had a spare moment—even for me."

Gregory planted both his feet on the porch, stopping the gentle sway of the swing. "Is that what you thought?" He turned to look at her.

She shrugged and continued to gaze out at the night as if the fireflies were blinking a Morse code that only she could understand. "It's no big deal," she muttered.

"Is that what you thought?" he repeated, laying a commanding hand on her arm.

She pulled her arm away. "What else was I supposed to think?"

"How about that I loved you? That you were the most important thing in the world to me?"

"I don't know why I would think that," Annabelle said in a brittle voice. She didn't want to say anything else, but she couldn't stop the words from pouring out. "I don't recall you ever standing up Greenpeace because you had a date with me or, being late for a nuclear disarmament rally because you'd agreed to meet me for a soda after pysch."

"This is why, isn't it?" he said softly, as if he was speaking to himself. "This is why."

"Why what?"

"This is why you left me. It is, isn't it, Annabelle?"

She got up from the swing and moved to the corner of the porch, leaning against the railing. Her arms wrapped around herself, she still refused to look at Gregory. She didn't want to do this. Didn't think she could stand it.

How was it possible that he hadn't realized why she'd left? It had never occurred to her that he'd been so involved in his causes that he honestly hadn't even realized what he was doing. Not that it

changed anything. Whether consciously or uncon-
sciously, she'd still come in second place.

"Gregory, I'm tired. I really don't want to go
over all this right now. It's nine-year-old business.
It doesn't matter anymore."

He stood and walked over to her, effectively
keeping her prisoner against the porch railing.
"This is why you left me, isn't it? Because somehow you felt you weren't as important to me as all
those other things."

She stared at him for a long moment, then said,
"Fine. You want the truth? You've got it. I felt like
all your causes were more important than I was. I
felt like I was in competition with Greenpeace and
Save the Bay and PETA and every other cause you
sank your teeth into. Only there never was any real
competition. I always came in second. Or third.
Somewhere behind the cause of the week."

Gregory looked stricken. "How could you
doubt what I felt for you?"

"I never knew what you felt for me. I knew you
wanted me. I knew you liked, even loved, having
sex with me, but that's all I knew."

"I loved you. I must have told you dozens of
times."

"Really? When?"

"I—I—didn't I?"

She shook her head. "Not once. Not even
once." She turned back to stare out into the dark
shadows of evening.

"I never told you?" Gregory sounded incredulous. "I thought those words so many times that I guess I just assumed—"

"It wouldn't have changed anything even if you had said the words. You'd have made the same choices and I'd have still felt like I wasn't important enough."

He put his hands on her shoulders and turned her back to face him. "Nothing was ever more important than you were. Nothing."

"Actions speak louder than words, Rev." The words weren't said accusatorily, they were simply stated, but Annabelle saw Gregory flinch as if he'd been struck. "You were always trekking off to one cause or the other and leaving me behind. Leaving me out."

"I'm sorry you felt that way, Annabelle. I never meant for—"

"It doesn't matter. It was over a long time ago."

"All these years I've wondered why you'd left. You never told me. Why didn't you even tell me? How could you love me and not tell me?"

Annabelle twisted out of his hands and hugged herself again. "It was because I loved you that I couldn't face you. I wasn't sure I could even say the words to you. I was afraid you'd talk me out of breaking up with you and I knew I couldn't go on living the way we were living. It's selfish, I know, and terribly egocentric, but I wanted to come first. I didn't want to have to vie for your attention with the environment and animal rights and human rights and civil rights."

"You never had to—"

"I had to all the time!" With an effort Annabelle lowered her voice. "Remember the concert we had tickets for? And you never showed up? How about the weekend of my sorority's spring formal? I'd bought a new dress, even spent a huge chunk of change getting my hair done. Where were you?"

"I couldn't help that. How was I to know that things would get a little out of hand at the rally?"

"What about the concert? You simply forgot that."

"Look, it was just a couple of times—"

"I don't know how many times I sat in the library waiting for you to show up and you didn't. And there were so many times when we were supposed to meet after class and you were held up at some meeting or another." She gave a tired sigh. "It happened all the time, Gregory."

He stared at her for a long time. "I—I don't know what to say. I'm sorry, Annabelle. I'm so sorry."

"It's over and done with, Gregory. We both made mistakes. Maybe I should have told you how I felt. And maybe you shouldn't have gotten involved with anyone until you'd gotten those causes out from under your skin."

"I believed—believe—in those causes, Annabelle. They were important then, and they're just as important now."

"I can see that. Even now, you're defending them to me."

"If no one fought for things, nothing would ever change," he said quietly.

"I know that too. I don't want to debate the issue with you. You asked a question and I answered it."

"I never meant to make you feel second best, Annie. You know that."

"Gregory, I really didn't want to rehash this. There's no use anyway. We can't change what happened."

"We need to—"

"We don't need to do anything, Rev. We really don't. I'm tired. And even if you did get a nice nap earlier today, you've got to be tired too. I'm going in now." She turned, but Gregory still stood in the way. With the porch railing on one side and the swing on the other, she couldn't go anywhere until he moved. "Gregory—"

"Not so fast. You don't want to talk about what happened anymore, so I'll respect your wishes. For the moment. But this isn't over, Annie. Not by a long shot."

"And like I told you before, I haven't been Annie for a long time. It's Annabelle."

"Okay. Annabelle. And like I told you, it's Gregory, not Rev."

She inclined her head. "Point taken."

He opened his mouth to say something else, but snapped it closed again and moved aside. "Good night, Annabelle."

She walked to the door and turned the doorknob, but before she could go inside, Gregory laid his hand on her arm. She sighed impatiently. "Gregory—"

"For your information, we never had sex, Annabelle. We made love. We made incredible love."

Her gaze locked with his for a long moment before she turned and went inside, closing the door behind her. Gregory stared at the blank door. Well, he'd wanted to know why she'd left him. Now he did. Somebody had once said, "Be careful what you wish for. You might get it." He'd gotten it all right. And he wished he hadn't.

All this time he'd thought it had been something else—that she'd fallen in love with another man, that she'd simply been too young to commit herself to one person. When she'd first left, he'd gone over his words and his actions with a fine-tooth comb time and again. He couldn't see that the blame might lie with him. He'd always sworn that he would have cut off his right arm rather than hurt her, but he'd hurt her anyway. However inadvertent, however unintentional his actions had been, he'd hurt her.

He started walking the same way they'd gone the other night and found himself back at Taylor's Rock. He climbed onto the boulder and sat, placing his hands in front of him, feeling the coolness of the stone. This was where he'd kissed her, where she'd kissed him back, where he'd felt the warm soft skin of her breasts against his chest, the sweet sweet taste of them in his mouth.

She'd made him forget that he was a minister with an image to uphold, an example to set. She'd made him forget anything and everything but that he was a man and she was a woman and that it felt good, and incredibly right, to hold her in his arms.

He propped his elbows on his knees and rested his forehead in his hands. He sat for what could have been minutes—or hours—frustrated, bewildered, hurting. Life had been so much simpler before Annabelle had come back. More boring, sure, and a lot lonelier, but simpler. Now it seemed as if she were systematically driving him insane—insane with the need to pull her into his arms and kiss her until she couldn't breathe, to love her until they were both too weak to walk.

Love her. That was the key. He still loved her. After nine years of growing up, changing, building different lives, he still loved her. No, that wasn't quite right. He'd loved her nine years ago, loved the sweet generous girl she'd been, loved the promise of the woman she'd be. Now he loved the woman she'd become. The thought gave him no joy, however. She didn't want his love. She seemed not to want anything from him at all.

Another mostly sleepless night. Annabelle woke up feeling as exhausted as she'd been when she'd crawled into bed. Why did it seem she'd have to leave town in order to get a decent night's sleep? At the very least, she'd just have to stay far, far away from the Reverend Gregory Talbott.

Easier said than done, though. She'd certainly see Gregory tonight at Daisy and Buddy's engagement party. She'd see him again tomorrow at church and Sunday dinner and the play. A few weeks from now there'd be the wedding rehearsal, and as a bridesmaid, she'd see him there too. Why did it seem as if the fates were conspiring against her?

She wanted to stay in White Creek, she really did. But she didn't know if she'd ever feel casual about running into Gregory. And it wasn't as if she could just stay away from church. This was a small town. The preacher was involved in so many things—the baseball games sponsored by the volunteer fire department, the beautification committee, and she knew Gregory headed up the annual fund drives for several charities. All this was complicated by the overwhelming realization that she didn't really want to stay away from him.

She sat up in bed and grimaced; she'd slept in her clothes again. This was getting to be a habit. Merlin, appearing from nowhere, jumped up on the bed, nestling down in the warm hollow she'd left in her pillow. "Okay, Merlin, you think you're so blasted smart, how do I handle this mess with

Gregory?" The cat gazed at her unblinkingly for a
moment, then turned his attention to grooming his
face, thoroughly ignoring her.

"I already tried ignoring him," she muttered.
"It's about as effective as trying to ignore an earth-
quake."

She heard the muffled peal of the doorbell and
the murmur of voices downstairs. By the way Merlin's ears pricked up as he jumped off the bed and
padded to the door, she knew it had to be Danni
and Sebastian. At least she was already dressed, she
thought ruefully, glancing down at her wrinkled
clothes. She tried pulling a brush through her tangled curls, winced a little, then gave up and fastened her hair at the nape of her neck with a clip.

She went downstairs and smiled as her cousin
Danielle was nearly engulfed by an enormous hug
from Gran. Danni, with her piquant face, long
blonde hair, and diminutive size looked about ten
years younger than her twenty-eight years.

"Hey, cuz," Annabelle called out. "You're fat."

Danni grinned and gave her swollen stomach a
fond pat. "Comes with the territory. Come here,
you." She tugged Annabelle to her for a hug.
"With twins, I expect I'll get a whole lot fatter before I get any thinner."

"I can't believe you're going to have twins."

"Neither can the doctor," Danni said dryly. "I
wasn't supposed to be able to get pregnant at all."

"But miracles happen every day." Sebastian
smiled.

Danni smiled at her husband, a smile so intimate that Annabelle felt as if she were intruding on
a private moment. She and Gregory used to smile
at each other that way. Dammit! No more, she
told herself. No more might-have-beens, no more
wondering, remembering, wishing. Only reality.
Only the here and now.

Sebastian turned his smile on Annabelle.
"How's it going, Annabelle? It's good to see you
again.

Annabelle eyed his dark-brown curls. "Hi, Sebastian. I see Danni finally talked you into growing
your hair a little. Looks good."

"And it only took five years," Danni murmured.

Sebastian rolled his eyes at Annabelle. "I got
tired of her nagging. So, how are you enjoying
your visit?"

Enjoying it? Annabelle thought. She felt as if
she'd been on more roller coasters than Disneyland had. "Fine," she said. "It's wonderful to
spend some time with Gran and to see all the
places Danni and I used to play as kids."

"How's Virgie holding up with the broken
arm?"

"Getting frustrated. She's not used to depend-
ing on anyone else. But she's okay. I have to ride
herd on her, though, to keep her from doing
things like washing Marigold with her cast on or
making tennis dates with Magda."

Sebastian grinned. "Sounds like Virgie." He

turned to his wife. "Danni, sweetheart, I'm going to take the suitcases back to the house and check with Grant to see about business. I'll come back for you in a little while."

"I can walk, you know. It's only a couple of blocks."

"I'll drive you home," Sebastian said with finality.

Danni sighed good-naturedly. "Yes, dear." When Sebastian opened the front door to leave, Merlin rose and trotted out, waiting for Sebastian to follow.

"Well, I know where his loyalties lie," Danni murmured. "And I'll remember those loyalties come suppertime," she called after the cat, then turned back to Annabelle. "Now tell the truth. How has it gone, really?"

Annabelle slumped down on the edge of the sofa. "It hasn't been easy. Seeing Gregory, I mean."

"I figured that. You look like you've barely slept at all, except that your clothes look like you slept in them."

"Yeah, I know. I've got so many bags beneath my eyes it looks like I'm packed for a trip around the world."

"Last time we talked, you said you weren't sure how you felt about Gregory, even after nine years. Do you know any better now?"

"God, no! All I know is that I don't know any

more than I did before. I think I know less. Things are all screwed up."

"Things? Or your feelings?"

Annabelle sighed. "Both. My feelings most of all."

"Why?"

"Darned if I know."

"It's because of the way you felt about him before?"

"Yes. No. I don't know. He's changed. So have I. But I do see little things that remind me of the way he used to be. It's like the past and the present are all mixed up together."

"Are you still in love with him?"

"After nine years? Like I said, he's not the same anymore. And I'm not either."

"So maybe you're in love with who he is now."

"Heaven forbid! It would never work. Never."

"You know," Danni said with a great deal of interest, "you certainly do protest vigorously."

"Yeah, I do, don't I? Do I sound convincing?"

"Not really."

"I didn't think so," Annabelle said morosely.

"I don't think I've ever seen you this rattled about anything before."

Wait around, Annabelle thought. It can only get worse.

NINE

Annabelle drove to Bosco's late that afternoon to get a package of bobby pins so she could put her hair up for the engagement party that night. When she walked back out to her car, she heard footsteps on the gravel behind her and knew it was Gregory. She didn't know how she knew. The small parking lot held about fifteen cars and was nearly always full, so it could have been anyone in the whole town of White Creek. But it was him.

"Hi, Rev," she said, without turning around.

She was surprised he let the "Rev" slip by, saying only, "You didn't lock your car door."

"Sorry," she said, waiting for the now familiar wariness to settle over her. It didn't. She'd been wearing caution like a cloak since coming back to White Creek and she wondered where it had gone. All she knew was that she was ridiculously glad to hear his voice.

"We need to talk," he said.

She had to agree. She'd said her piece last night, gotten nine years worth of baggage out of her system. But she hadn't given him a chance to say very much. She owed it to him to hear him out. "Okay. Here?"

"My house might be better."

"Shall I meet you there?"

"Can I ride with you?"

"I'm not planning on skipping out on you, Gregory."

He smiled. "I'll meet you there."

When Annabelle pulled up in front of Gregory's white frame house, he was right behind her. He walked up the sidewalk ahead of her and held the door for her to go inside.

She perched nervously on the edge of the sofa. What had put that serious, almost somber, look on his face? Was he going to tell her that he'd gotten the past out of his system, that he was now ready to move on with his life—without her? "Okay, so let's talk," she said.

"I'll bring you something to drink. Iced tea okay?"

She nodded. "Fine. Unsweetened. Do you have lemon?"

"You didn't used to take lemon."

"And I used to take it loaded with sugar. I guess my taste buds have grown up." *Dammit, let's get on with this!*

"Along with the rest of you," he murmured, and went into the kitchen.

Annabelle sat on the sofa and stared at the PETA poster directly opposite her. RESPECT YOUR FELLOW EARTHLINGS. She'd noticed at Sunday dinners that he ate helpings of everything except the meat. She figured he'd gone vegetarian, though he never said anything and never called attention to it. She had to give him that. He didn't just pay lip service when he stood up for a cause. He meant it, believed it, practiced what he preached.

"Here." He handed her a tall glass of tea and sat next to her on the sofa. She hadn't expected that. She'd figured he'd sit in his recliner. Sipping her tea, she analyzed the frisson of awareness that shivered up her spine. Nope, it still wasn't wariness. This was more along the lines of pure sensual energy—the female radar in her honing in on his male presence.

She waited for him to say something, but he simply drank his tea, then gazed at the ice cubes in his glass as if they held the answers to the secrets of the universe.

She couldn't wait any longer. She had to know where things stood between them. "Gregory?"

He sighed heavily. "I'm sorry, Annabelle. I know I keep saying that, but I want to know what I have to do to make you realize that I mean it with all my heart."

"Sorry?"

"For messing up back in college. For not realizing that you have to work at having a relationship. For letting you think, for even one second, that you weren't the most important thing in the world to me. Take your pick."

Annabelle felt her heartbeat slow at his softly spoken words. For some crazy reason, she was afraid she might cry. She should tell him that it had happened a long time ago and didn't matter anymore. She should. But she didn't. Because suddenly it mattered very much to her that he had apologized. What had happened last night had changed everything. Somehow, in airing out all the old hurt, most of it had dissipated, leaving her feeling strangely free.

"I'm sorry, too, Gregory. I wasn't very good at relationships either and I guess I should have told you I was feeling neglected."

He stared at his ice cubes awhile longer, then looked at her long enough to say, "It's been good to get to know you again. You're an incredible woman." He went back to watching his ice cubes melt.

"I . . . well, it's been good to get to know you again. You've become quite a minister." Now she was the one staring at her ice cubes.

"I'm also a man, Annabelle. A man who wants very much to spend time with you. To work at a relationship with you. Could we try it again? Could we try and see if we can get it right this time?"

She turned to him and saw a look of such longing on his face, it hurt her. It also scared her. "I—I don't know what to say."

"Don't say anything. You don't have to answer at all. We can just take it a day at a time."

She looked back down at her hands, which were clutching her glass so tightly, her fingertips were white from the pressure. "A day at a time," she echoed.

She felt Gregory's fingertip glide down her cheek to her chin, then lift it so she could meet his gaze. He brushed his lips across hers, a light, sweet, nonthreatening kiss. "One hour at a time, if that's what you want." He kissed her again, with exquisite tenderness.

"I, uh, suppose we could do that. An hour at a time," she hastened to add. "No strings, no promises."

"No strings, no promises." *At least no strings tying you to me*, Gregory thought. *I'm already tied to you in the most binding of ways.* He brushed one more kiss across her lips and grinned. "Since we're going to take it an hour at a time, can I have you for the next hour?"

She smiled back. "I have to get ready for the engagement party."

"Shall I pick you up?"

"I've already made arrangements to ride with Danni and Sebastian. I suppose I could call them—no, I'll just meet you there."

"Fine. But tell them you have another ride

home." He tilted his head to one side, his gaze holding hers.

"I . . . Okay."

Gregory escorted her to her car, opened the door for her, then bent to kiss her again. He shut her car door, then tapped on her car window and pointed at the lock.

He grinned as she stuck out her tongue, even as she locked her car door and drove off.

Gregory smiled and chatted, saying all the right things, but his attention was focused on the door. Annabelle, with Danni and Sebastian, would be there any minute. It would be nice to see Danni and Sebastian—he and Sebastian had become good friends in the five years since Sebastian had moved to White Creek. But it wasn't Danni and Sebastian who had his heart pounding when they walked in the door. It was Annabelle.

She was dressed in a turquoise halter-top sundress that made the creamy skin of her arms and shoulders glow in contrast. Her hair was pinned on top of her head, but dozens, even hundreds, of curly tendrils escaped to caress her forehead and the nape of her neck. She flashed a shy but sweet smile in his direction before being swallowed up by a swarm of women.

"No strings, no promises," he said under his breath, then repeated it for good measure. Easier said than done, he realized, when what he really wanted to do was take her home and promise to make love to her all night, then keep that promise.

"So how's it goin', Greg?"

Gregory turned to see Sebastian had joined him. "Welcome back, Sebastian. How was Disneyland?"

"I went nuts trying to keep Danni off most of the rides, but it's always nice getting away with her. So what's been going on around here the past couple of weeks?"

Gregory caught him up on the news of the town, though his gaze seldom left Annabelle as she laughed and talked with Magda's daughters. Sebastian went into more detail about his vacation, and Gregory listened with half an ear while watching Bosco Wilson's older son, Jimmy, who was visiting from Maryland, put the moves on Annabelle.

Gregory's hands tightened into fists and didn't relax until she laughingly rebuffed Jimmy, leaving him to wander off to try his wiles on Caterina. Only then did he turn his attention back to Sebastian's conversation.

". . . and we left the purple-haired quadruplets in the care of their nanny so we could be here tonight."

"What?"

"I thought that might get your attention. It took longer than I expected, though. I think Annabelle can breathe, even if you don't watch her every breath."

"Sorry, I—"

"I've been there, ol' friend. A word to the wise. Don't fight it."

"I'm not. *She* is."

Sebastian grimaced in sympathy. "Sorry, I can't help you there. With Danni and me, it was mostly me who was stubborn and hardheaded. Why don't you go over and say hello? It's not like you're hearing a whole lot of what I'm saying."

Gregory thought for all of a tenth of a second before heading in Annabelle's direction. Oh God, he thought, the White Shoulders was back in full force. He noticed her scent as he came up behind her. "You smell good," he murmured in her ear. "And you look even better."

She turned and smiled at him. "You don't look so bad yourself, Rev."

Gregory stayed by her side for most of the party. It rapidly became obvious to everyone there that he considered her his territory. Jimmy, shot down by Caterina, came back around and was subjected to positively threatening looks.

"Jeez, I thought you're supposed to be a preacher," Jimmy grumbled.

"I am a preacher," Gregory said. He smiled pleasantly and spoke softly so Annabelle wouldn't hear. "I am also a man with a jealous streak and a short fuse. Annabelle is mine. Enjoy the party."

"What was that all about?" Annabelle asked, when she'd finished her conversation with Lily Jones.

"Nothing important," Gregory assured her.

"Just a male thing." He ran a possessive gaze over her hair, wondering how many pins he'd have to remove to tumble the soft curls down around her shoulders—those temptingly bare shoulders.

If he pressed kisses on her back starting with her left shoulder blade, he wondered how many kisses it would take to get to her right shoulder blade. And if he kissed those perfectly lipsticked lips, how many kisses would it take before he'd kissed all the lipstick off, before he went completely over the edge? Not many, he suspected. He wanted to find out.

But more than anything, he wanted to know what it would take to persuade Annabelle to give them another chance. He didn't just want an hour or a day. He wanted what his lack of understanding had cost them. He wanted the rest of her life.

She was still attracted to him. He'd have to be an idiot not to see that. And he believed her feelings went beyond the physical. Her actions spoke so much more loudly than words. She had stayed with him when he needed someone; she worried about him. He needed to know how deep her feelings went. He doubted they went as deep as his, but he could work on that.

Right now he had to get her out of there. He couldn't work on the rest of her life until he had her undivided attention. He figured they couldn't be the first to leave, but they'd darn well be the second.

Sebastian and Danni were the first to leave—

over Danni's halfhearted protests—with Sebastian insisting that she was sleeping for three now. Gregory and Annabelle left a few minutes later, after a discreet good-bye to Daisy and Buddy.

"You want to tell me why you insisted we had to leave now?" Annabelle asked as Gregory helped her into his car.

"I have a surprise for you."

"I love surprises. What is it?"

"If I told you, then it wouldn't be a surprise, now would it?"

"I guess not. So when do I get it?"

"In a few minutes."

"Where is it?"

"At my house."

Annabelle had a strong feeling that this was all just a ruse to be alone with her, but couldn't find it in herself to be upset. As a matter of fact, she really wanted to have a chance to test this new truce of theirs. She had never thought that it would actually help to tell Gregory how she felt, but it had. And it had helped even more to have Gregory acknowledge what had happened and apologize for it. Just to know that he hadn't consciously relegated her to secondary importance made a big difference.

And now Gregory was older and wiser, certainly more focused. After all, she'd been here over two weeks and he hadn't attended a single rally or demonstration. Maybe he just paid his membership dues and let someone else do all the work. She could live with that. Or maybe he could stick to one or two causes at a time instead of feeling like he had to take on the problems of the whole world.

She sat on his sofa, her eyes closed as he had instructed her. She heard the music of the Magic Monkeys, a quasi-hard-rock band she'd claimed was her favorite back in college—but not for one second afterward—then Gregory told her to open her eyes. On the coffee table in front of her was a beautiful silver bowl piled high with fresh June strawberries and a saucer of powdered sugar for dipping, along with two tall glasses of what she strongly suspected was root beer.

This used to be a favorite study method for the two of them. They'd munch on strawberries or some other fruit and drink gallons of root beer while listening to the Magic Monkeys. Only now she'd outgrown the Magic Monkeys, she was allergic to strawberries, and she hated—no, loathed—root beer.

She smiled weakly. "Oh. How . . . nice." He looked so pleased that she forced herself to pick up her glass and take a cautious sip. Yes, it was root beer. And yes, it tasted awful. She avoided a grimace only with an effort and a reminder that he thought he was being sweet. No, he *was* being sweet. It wasn't his fault he'd missed the target altogether.

She wasn't sure what she was going to do about the strawberries, though. She could try to tune out the Magic Monkeys, she could choke down the root beer, but if she ate a strawberry, she'd swell up like a balloon. Still, a funny feeling tickled the pit of her stomach and she didn't think it had anything to do with the root beer she'd drunk. It had to do with Gregory's obvious effort to create a special treat for her.

"Thank you, Gregory," she said softly. "This is lovely."

"So have a strawberry."

"Um, I sort of pigged out on the veggies and dip at the party. I'm really not very hungry. But this is very sweet of you."

He started to speak, but at that moment she winced when the Magic Monkeys went into a particularly loud—and lousy—drum solo. She tried to cover it up with another smile, but wound up laughing instead. "Oh Gregory," she gasped, "I had forgotten just how truly awful they were."

He smiled ruefully. "They were pretty bad, weren't they? I guess that part of the surprise fell through, didn't it?"

She reached out and laid a hand on his. "To be brutally honest, I can't stand root beer anymore and I've developed an allergy to strawberries. That doesn't mean I don't appreciate the thought that went into this."

He sighed. "So I blew it, huh?"

She nodded. "But in a very sweet way. Gregory, you don't need to bring up reminders of the past. Why don't we just worry about the future instead?"

"I thought you'd never ask." He turned off the music and blessed silence reigned as he sat next to her on the sofa, draping his arm around her shoulders. "Speaking of futures, have you given any more thought to ours?"

She cast a quick glance at him, but he was gazing across the room at a huge color poster of the Greenpeace ship, *The Rainbow Warrior*. His voice sounded as offhand as if he'd just asked her what time it was.

"I, um, thought that this hour-at-a-time thing sounded fine."

"I want more time than an hour." He still sounded as casual as if they were involved in nothing more than party chatter.

"How much more time?" This time Annabelle gazed at the poster.

The arm around her shoulders became less casual and more purposeful as it tugged her closer. She could feel his warm breath on her ear and the sharp, but pleasant nip of teeth on her earlobe.

"A day?" Her voice was husky.

His free hand brushed tendrils of her hair aside as his lips trailed kisses down her neck. "More," he murmured against her skin.

She turned her face toward his, and the trail of kisses abruptly reversed direction and headed up to the corner of her mouth. He ran the tip of his tongue over her bottom lip, then sucked it gently into his mouth.

"A—a week?" Her voice had become weak,

thready, and her head seemed to be floating about twelve inches above her body. "Two weeks?"

"Longer." She could feel his warm breath against her mouth.

"I, ah, don't know." She angled her whole body toward him. "You could . . . mm . . . persuade me. Maybe."

"I love persuading," Gregory murmured, moving closer. He nibbled all around her lips before taking her mouth in earnest. He kissed her as though it were his first time—sweetly, with a passion that was both innocent and earthy. He kissed as if it were his last time—with raw, blinding need.

He pulled back and searched her face again, only this time the question in his eyes was different from all the times before. The question was full of tender need and a yearning that was pure and perfect. "I don't want an hour or a day or a week or even a year. I want the rest of our lives."

Her heart pounded so loudly, she wasn't sure she'd heard him. "Gregory?"

"I want all the time we've missed. I know it's crazy. I know it's too damn soon and I know you need time. I'll give you time, sweetheart. I'll give you all the time you need, but you need to know where I'm heading. I want to marry you."

"Gregory?" This time she felt her lips form the word, but knew no sound came out. God, yes, it was crazy and too damn soon. And, yes, she needed more time. "I—I need time."

"But you're not saying no."

She smiled and whispered, "I'm not saying no."

"Annabelle, I love you."

For a man capable of such eloquence, she thought, the words were amazingly simple. And incredibly moving.

"I love you too."

A primitive man would have hauled her off to his cave, an impatient man would have pushed her down on the sofa to stake his claim. Gregory was both civilized and patient. He simply kissed her senseless. Slow kisses, deep kisses, wet kisses. She shivered in his arms and opened her mouth wider to his.

He didn't think he'd ever tasted anything as wonderful as her. He was addicted to the taste, intoxicated with the feeling. He explored her ear, relished the pulse at the base of her throat, savored the curve of her shoulders. He pushed her back on the sofa and untied her sundress, then pushed the top down an inch to reveal her upper breasts. He lowered it another inch and tasted the valley between them. He tugged it down to her waist and took her tight rosy nipples into his mouth.

Annabelle gasped and sighed and moaned with pleasure, inciting him to taste more. More. If he was intoxicated with the taste and feel of her, she was high on the taste and feel of him. She felt as if she'd been empty, so empty, for nine years and only now was the emptiness being filled. She drank in the sweetness of his lips on hers, craved the feel of his silky hair beneath her fingers, needed his clean scent filling her nostrils when she closed her eyes.

And yet, when his caresses slowed, then stilled, when his mouth left her breasts and pressed one more kiss on her lips before he pulled away, she didn't stop him. She couldn't honestly say she wanted him to stop, but things were moving a little too fast.

He chuckled ruefully. "I think we'd better stop before you make me forget all my good intentions. You could tempt a saint beyond redemption, sweetheart."

Annabelle blushed as she fumbled with the top of her dress.

"Turn around and let me tie that for you."

"I seem to be all thumbs," she said and did as he requested.

He kissed the back of her neck before retying the straps to her sundress. "I'll run you home."

"Could we walk?" Annabelle asked.

"I'd love to." The moon was just a few days past full and still shone down brightly, glinting off her hair. Gregory tucked his arm securely around her waist and looked down at her. Her hair was tousled beyond repair, most of the bobby pins having been pulled out when Gregory had tunneled his fingers through her hair. Her lips were red and slightly puffy. Her dress was hopelessly wrinkled and he'd even tied it lopsided at the back. She looked like a woman who'd been thoroughly, passionately, loved. And the sight excited him all over again.

Gregory kissed her on her front porch and she leaned into him, sighing. "Gregory, can I ask you something?"

"Anything."

"You said that, well, you believed that sex was okay outside of marriage if there was commitment."

"Yes."

"Then why didn't you make love to me tonight?" Her voice was tinged with desire and frustration.

Gregory kissed her again, then leaned back to hold her gaze with his. "For one thing, even though I am committed to you, heart and soul, you haven't committed to me yet. More important than that, though, is the way I feel about you. When I marry you, I want to be able to seal that contract in the most sacred way God intended for man and woman to seal any marriage." He grinned. "And since I intend to marry you very soon after you say yes, I don't intend to have to wait that long, anyway."

He kissed her once more, then turned to leave. She stood and watched him walk away, slowly, reluctantly, as if he didn't want to leave. He looked back several times and smiled at her. She smiled back and continued to smile until he disappeared into the night shadows.

TEN

Annabelle didn't sleep any better that night than she had the previous nights, but it was a delicious insomnia filled with mental replays of the evening spent in Gregory's arms, tempered with a little frustration that she wasn't *still* in his arms. Okay, a lot of frustration.

Underlying everything was a nudge of uneasiness. Things had changed so dramatically in such a short time. When she thought of his kisses and caresses, she couldn't believe he'd ever relegate her to second place again, but her better sense told her to put off giving him a definite answer for a while.

She didn't hear a word he said during church the next morning. She kept looking at the man wearing a black robe and seeing, instead, the man who'd held her in his arms and driven her mad with desire. Maybe church wasn't the right place to be thinking such things, she thought guiltily, but the way he made her feel *was* heavenly.

After the service, she and her grandmother walked to the back of the church with everyone else. When it was her turn to shake Gregory's hand, Annabelle leaned close and whispered, "Great sermon, Rev."

He gave her an intimate smile that sent her blood pressure up a few points, then said politely, "See you at dinner." His eyes, though, were not polite at all. They were wicked and wanton and blatantly said he wished *she* was dinner.

Annabelle couldn't recall having a better Sunday dinner. She had her grandmother to thank, bless her unsubtle heart. As soon as everyone was done eating, she abruptly stood and all but pushed Danni and Sebastian out the door, saying Danni needed a nap. Then she grabbed Lute by the hand and said they were going back to Lute's house. Another transparently obvious ploy to leave her and Gregory alone, Annabelle thought. This time she didn't mind at all.

No sooner had Virgie and Lute headed off in Lute's beat-up truck, than Gregory tugged Annabelle into his arms for a kiss, then another and another. He kissed her until she thought she'd melt in his arms. He kissed her until they both gasped for air, then he drew back to suck in a deep breath. "Maybe we should go take care of the dishes," he said. "It would be safer."

"So who wants to be safe?"

He laughed and picked her up, carrying her into the kitchen and letting her slide to her feet in front of the sink.

"Ah," she said, "I suspected you were the sort who wanted his women in the kitchen or the bedroom."

"In the bedroom, sweetheart. In the bedroom. Anyway, this is dangerous territory. Now hush and do the dishes. I'll dry."

However, as soon as Annabelle put her hands in the dishwater, Gregory took unfair advantage and lifted her hair to press kisses along the back of her neck. He skimmed his hands along her sides, resting for a moment on the curve of her hips, then slid his hands back up. "Have I told you how much I love this silky red top?" he breathed into her ear.

"You always did like me in red," she murmured, her voice catching as he moved his hands around front and cupped her breasts.

"I always liked you best out of it," he growled as his fingers plucked at her rapidly hardening nipples. He grasped the hem of her top and lifted it over her head, then unfastened her bra so her breasts could spill into his hands.

She moaned, closing her eyes at the incredible feelings. "God, Gregory, who's venturing into dangerous territory now?"

He didn't answer, preoccupied with kissing her back, from one shoulder blade to the other, while his hands caressed her breasts.

When she leaned back against him, he turned her to face him, his eyes darkening almost to black as his gaze lingered on her creamy breasts and rosy nipples. He cupped her breasts again and whispered, "I feel like my hands have been empty for nine years." He kissed her once more. "And I feel like my heart has been empty for nine years."

Annabelle clung to him to keep her weakening knees from buckling beneath her, her wet hands leaving damp spots on his cotton shirt. His body urged hers back against the kitchen counter, his denim-covered erection pressing into her abdomen.

"Are you trying to drive me insane?" she whispered against his mouth.

"I think I'm driving myself insane," he muttered and lifted her, sitting her on the edge of the kitchen table. He kissed her again, heady dark kisses of need. How did he know what she wanted, needed, almost before she did? Just when she thought she'd go crazy if she didn't feel his lips on her breasts, he took a nipple into his mouth. Just when she thought she couldn't last another minute without touching his warm hard flesh, he tugged his shirt over his head so she could caress her fingers up and down his back. He urgently pushed her skirt to her waist and ran seeking hands over her thighs.

And just when she knew she couldn't feel any more intensely than she already did, he slid off her panties and stroked her moist heat, proving that she could. He petted and teased and tasted, and through the haze of feelings that surrounded her, nearly consuming her, flowed soft sweet words of love and need, heady promises of commitment and possession.

With his fingers he brought her to the edge, with his lips he nudged her over. When she had cried out in ecstasy while her body was still quivering, he took her mouth again.

He drew in a deep breath and kissed her one more time. He tugged the skirt of her dress down to cover her.

"We'd better stop while we still can."

"You're right," she murmured, leaning her forehead against his chest. "Things are moving kind of fast."

"I know, sweetheart," Gregory whispered and kissed her briefly, but thoroughly, his lips lingering as if they didn't want to release her. "And at the same time not nearly fast enough. What I really want to do is carry you off to my bed and show you in a dozen different ways how much I want you. How much I love you." He drew in a deep breath and stepped away from her long enough to hunt down the bra and silk top he'd tossed aside just minutes before. "That's what I want to do. What I'm going to do is help you get dressed, then keep my hands to myself before we set off the smoke detector."

Gregory dressing her was almost as sexy as him undressing her. Almost. He drew the bra over her arms, then smoothed the lacy cups in place before he fastened it. He gently tugged the silk top over her head a little at a time, kissing first her forehead, then her nose, then her chin as each was exposed. They were both breathing heavily by the time she was fully clothed.

They spent the remainder of the afternoon sitting on the porch swing—Gregory swore it was safer sitting out in the open—and catching up on all the years they'd been apart. Annabelle shook her head at some of Gregory's stories about a young minister fresh out of seminary, who was unconventional at the best of times, trying to fit into his first church—a most conventional church in northern Virginia.

She smiled at the thought of a younger Gregory showing up for a church cookout in shorts and tennis shoes, only to be sent home like a recalcitrant child to change into long pants. Ministers weren't supposed to show their legs. Thank heavens White Creek allowed their ministers to be human, she thought.

They talked about books, music, politics, economics, philosophy. They talked as if trying to cover nine years' worth of changes in one afternoon. They talked while they fixed and ate a light supper. They sat down to watch a movie on television and talked through that. They talked long after Virgie came home and went to bed. They talked until Virgie poked her head around the top of the stairs during a highly charged political discussion and asked them to hold it down.

Then they whispered. Except that Gregory loved her throaty breathless-sounding whispers and wound up kissing her—which left her breathless for real. Finally, reluctantly, Gregory went home.

Annabelle went to Gregory's Monday to fix dinner—or rather, to have him show her how to fix a vegetarian lentil-mushroom loaf with herb gravy. Not only was the food good, but Gregory was outstanding in the kitchen, better than she was. She didn't mind. As long as he did most of the cooking, she wouldn't even mind eating vegetarian. He kept his house clean but not antiseptic, just the way she kept her place. Maybe she had on rose-colored glasses, but it was beginning to seem that time had turned Gregory into the perfect man.

After dinner, they left the dishes in the sink and sat on the sofa kissing. "Should we be doing this?" Annabelle murmured as his lips nibbled around her ear.

"Probably not. We're definitely playing with dynamite, don't you think?"

"Oh yes." She sighed as he ran a finger around the neck of her scoop-neck T-shirt. "Yes, we're definitely—what did you call it?—venturing into dangerous territory here."

"So let's walk the line." Gregory slid his hands

beneath the hem of her shirt, then groaned in frustration when the telephone rang. "Just as well," he said. "It's getting too warm in here anyway."

He dashed into the kitchen and grabbed the phone on the fourth ring, then came out a few minutes later. "I'm sorry, sweetheart, but I need to meet with the McKinleys for a little while this evening. A family problem. I'll take you back to your grandmother's."

Annabelle tried to hide her disappointment. "No. I'll stay here and wash the dishes and maybe you'll get home before too late."

"Leave the dishes. I'll do them later, but I'd love to find you here when I get home."

"I'll do the dishes. After all, you cooked most of the dinner. Go on. I'll wait."

And wait she did. Nine o'clock. Ten o'clock. Eleven o'clock. Midnight. She was awakened by the barest touches on her face—a butterfly wing, a feather, angel hair. She opened her eyes to find Gregory's face inches away, his gaze soft as he watched her. He pressed a kiss on the tip of her nose. "I'm sorry for being so long, sweetheart."

"That's okay." She gave him a sleepy smile. "What time is it?"

"About one. Come on, I'll take you home. I'm really sorry this ruined our evening, though. I'll make it up to you tomorrow night, okay? Whoops, not tomorrow night. I'm going to the Missionary Society's slide show of missionaries in Brazil. Tomorrow for lunch, then. I'll take you to the newest restaurant in town, the Tastee Burger."

"Do they have something there you can eat?" she asked around a yawn.

"I usually order the Tastee Burger Deluxe— minus the burger. They don't mind. And they only charge me half price since they leave off the meat. I'll pick you up about eleven-thirty."

Halfway through lunch, Charlotte McKinley came into the Tastee Burger, her eyes red-rimmed. Gregory sat with her at another table talking while Annabelle stirred her melting milkshake with her straw and patiently watched his cheese fries get cold and gummy. It could be worse, she decided. He could have raced off to a demonstration.

He came over to her a few minutes later and said, "Do you mind driving yourself home? You can take my car. Charlotte will give me a ride home later and I'll walk over to pick it up. I'm sorry, sweetheart." He handed her his keys and gave her a quick kiss. "I'll call you tonight after the meeting."

Oh well, she thought as she drove home. She had to figure something like this would happen once in a while. When he'd left the night before, she'd wandered around his little house, curious about the man she'd so quickly fallen in love with again. When she'd opened the door of his study, she'd seen two solid walls of built-in bookshelves full of books on counseling.

And she'd seen something else that had surprised her. A degree in counseling from the university in Norfolk. She'd never thought about it before, but she guessed counseling was an important part of being a minister. It couldn't have been easy being a full-time minister as well as a part-time student. His dedication impressed her.

He called her that night after the meeting and she lay in her bed talking to him, wishing she was lying in *his* bed talking to him. Still, their conversation was sweet and satisfying. Not as satisfying as being with him, but satisfying anyway. And he promised her he'd come by Wednesday night after choir practice was over.

Wednesday night they cuddled in front of the television, fought over popcorn, and shared buttery kisses. The tension that had begun to creep in around the edges of Annabelle's thoughts receded.

Until Thursday night. Gregory took her to a new seafood restaurant he'd heard about in Norfolk, but no sooner had they walked in the door and given the hostess his name than she gave him a message from Virgie. Annabelle could tell it wasn't good news by the look on his face. "I'm sorry, sweetheart. We've got to go back. It's the McKinleys again."

She forced a smile. "No problem, Gregory. Maybe we can try this again tomorrow night."

"I'd love to, sweetheart, but I'm speaking at a rally over in Waverly at seven. I'll come by afterward."

"Sure."

He cupped her face. "Look, it's not like it was before. I promise. But Fleurique, a cosmetic company that tests on animals, is considering building a plant near Waverly. It's important to let them know what they're up against."

Annabelle smiled again and nodded, but the uneasiness was back. She tried to push it aside, to ignore it, but it was getting harder to do.

Saturday night they had a wonderful dinner at Danni and Sebastian's, and Annabelle found it easier to gloss over her doubts—though they didn't go away. Still, it was good to see Gregory and Sebastian joke around and kid each other. It showed her another side to Gregory that she'd almost missed—a funny, whimsical side. It was real easy to fall in love with that side too.

Sunday he didn't come for dinner because he had to drive back to Waverly after church for a meeting regarding Fleurique. He showed up midafternoon and took her for a drive to the beach. They held hands and walked on the sand for hours. When the sun went down, they sat on the cool sand and cuddled. But when Gregory brought up his proposal of marriage, Annabelle sidetracked him with kisses. She wasn't ready to discuss that just yet.

The next week was more of the same. Monday, Gregory headed up the new youth outreach meeting. Tuesday he spent visiting various congregation members who were housebound for one reason or another. Wednesday night he had choir practice, though he came by afterward for a couple of hours. Thursday night was another Stop Fleurique meeting and Friday night was another meeting with the McKinleys after a quick trip into Tidewater with Lily Jones to meet with someone from the Save the Bay Foundation. And, of course, he was in his church office every day from nine to two—except Wednesdays when he volunteered at a homeless shelter in Norfolk.

Annabelle tried to be understanding and supportive, she really did. She tried to grin and bear it, but it got harder and harder to grin without clenching her teeth. To make things worse, she was getting the unsettling feeling that this wasn't just a flux. This was normal. Yet when she brought up the Save the Bay Foundation and the Stop Fleurique campaign, he insisted those were especially urgent things that needed his attention.

The spare minutes she did spend with Gregory were wonderful. She wasn't just in love with him; he'd rapidly become her best friend as well. They could talk for hours—when he had time to talk— and never run out of things to say, yet they were both equally comfortable sitting together in companionable silence. Of course, permeating everything was the passion that simmered just beneath the surface, constantly threatening to bubble over.

The following Monday, Annabelle showed up at Gregory's at ten. He'd left the church secretary holding down the fort for the day and intended to take Annabelle into Richmond to see the museum and a botanical garden. As they left, the phone rang.

"Don't answer it," Annabelle said. "Come on, let's go."

Gregory grimaced. "I'm sorry, sweetheart. I won't be but a minute."

I'm sorry, sweetheart. She sure seemed to hear those words a lot these days, she thought, her face wrinkling into a frown. When Gregory came back into the room, she quickly smoothed her features and put on a smile, then it, too, faded when she saw his face. "What's wrong?"

"It's Hilary Cochran. She's had another heart attack and she's going into surgery for a quadruple bypass in a little while."

"So you're going to the hospital."

He nodded.

"Then I'll go with you."

"Thanks, sweetheart. It'll help to have you there."

Last time Annabelle had been in the Norfolk hospital, it had been a long, long night. This, she could tell, would be a long, long day. Mrs. Cochran's daughter, Pat, and her husband had been staying in White Creek since Mrs. Cochran had come home from the hospital, so they were right there. Her son was flying in again from Ohio.

Annabelle once more marveled at Gregory and how unfailingly supportive and caring he was with Pat and Tim. He talked with them, prayed with them, even made phone calls for them. After several hours he finally came back over to sit next to Annabelle.

"How're you holding up?" he asked. "Okay?"

She nodded. "What's going on?"

"No news yet. It'll be another hour or two before the surgery's over and we'll just have to wait and see what happens. Pat's feeling a little guilty, I think. She's afraid she was letting her mother do too much. I told her that the person hadn't been born who could keep Hilary from doing what she wants to do."

"I'm sure that helped. Are you holding up okay?"

He smiled wearily. "I guess. At least this isn't the crack of dawn."

"That's right. You never were much of a morning person, were you?"

"I'm still not. And, luckily, I don't usually have to be up too early. Sunday mornings I'm up by eight, at church by nine. During the week, the same thing. The only time I get up earlier than that is Easter morning for the sunrise service. I don't mind that because sunrise on Easter morning is as full of magic as Christmas morning. More so, because Christmas gave us a baby, Easter gave us a miracle." He smiled again, then stood. "I'm going to the hospital chapel. I'll be back in a few minutes."

Ten minutes later she went to find him. When she opened the chapel door, she saw him on his knees in front of the altar. His hands were resting on the polished oak railing and his face was lifted up as he prayed silently. When he was finished, a look of absolute peace settled over him.

Funny, she thought as she saw the serenity that suffused his face. When she'd met him, he'd believed in God, but he'd never been especially religious. She knew that he had to have a deep belief in order to become a minister, but she was suddenly seeing just how deep that faith went. It was an uncompromising, all-encompassing faith, and it disconcerted her as nothing else had.

Up until now she'd been thinking of his ministry as just another one of his causes. Now she saw that it was more. So much more.

Thinking back over the past couple of weeks, she realized that he was on call almost like a doctor. Didn't a minister have to contend with evenings spent visiting members of the congregation? And what about Saturdays spent preparing sermons or performing weddings? How about being called any hour of the day or night to counsel people or comfort them? Or how about having your own life be an open book, above reproach? One slipup, one indication that you might be just an average guy, could cost you your job.

Her heart slammed in her chest and her palms grew damp. How could she have been so unobservant? So blind? What a fool's paradise she'd been living in! Her stomach churned and she stared at Gregory's strong and precious features as he slowly got to his feet.

Dear God, she loved him, but she didn't think she could compete with this cause. She'd always felt neglected because of his dedication, but this wasn't just dedication. This was devotion. And this wasn't just a cause. This was his life.

Annabelle and Gregory stayed until they knew Hilary Cochran had come through the surgery with flying colors. When they arrived back in White Creek, Gregory automatically headed his car toward his house, only Annabelle stopped him. "Gregory, I have a little headache. Would you mind taking me to Gran's?"

"Are you sure you don't want to come to my house? I'll fix you something to eat and massage your shoulders."

God, that sounded good. She could almost feel his talented fingers working the kinks out of her body. She just didn't think he'd be able to work the kinks out of her thoughts as well. "No, thanks anyway. I think I'll just lie down for a while and take a nap." *Please, just hurry and get me home. I'm being held together by only a couple of safety pins right now and I need to fall apart alone.*

"Well, if you're sure . . ." he began, disappointment edging his voice.

"I'm sure." No sooner had his car stopped in front of her grandmother's house than Annabelle headed up the walk. She went straight to her bedroom and closed the door carefully, then sat on the bed. She looked down at her hands, surprised to see them clenched in her lap. She loosened them and was even more surprised to see them tremble.

It wasn't going to work. She knew that as clearly as if it were written on the wall across from her. Why hadn't she realized it before now? Had she been so intrigued with the new feelings blossoming between them that she'd ignored everything else? Or was it that she just hadn't *wanted* to notice?

She curled up in a ball on her bed, her thoughts spinning until she felt dizzy and sick. Her throat felt tight, her eyes burned and stung. Then she cried. She cried softly so that her grandmother wouldn't hear. She cried for all the hurt she'd gone through nine years ago. She cried for the hurt she'd endured between then and now. And she cried most of all for how much it was going to hurt when she left him. Again.

What upset her the most was that she was going to hurt him too. And it really wasn't his fault. She wished, with all her heart, that he'd find someone who could love him without reservations, could be there for him, stand by him, and not mind not being first with him. More than anything, she wished she could be that person. She couldn't, though.

She skipped supper and stayed in her room, staring off into space, trying desperately not to think. Finally she slept and slept deeply, dreamlessly, but awoke feeling as weary as if she hadn't slept at all.

Gregory called her about ten and she had to take a deep breath to keep the tears at bay. "I'm fine," she told him. "My headache's gone." Just not the heartache, she thought.

"Are you sure, sweetheart? You don't sound like yourself."

"I'm fine. Really."

"Okay, then." His voice sounded doubtful. "I'll come by after two."

"No. I'll meet you at church."

"But why?"

"I just want to. Okay?"

"Sure. Whatever you want is fine with me."

Annabelle hung up the receiver and had to force her hand to release it. She was going to have to talk to him that afternoon; that was why she wanted to meet him at the church. It was more neutral territory than her grandmother's house. And she really didn't want memories of Gregory's hurt haunting Gran's living room.

She arrived at the church at two on the button, just as Barbara Jennings, the part-time church secretary, was leaving. Annabelle forced herself to smile and chat politely for a minute, until Barbara glanced at her watch and hurried out, saying she needed to be home before her son got out of school. Once she'd left, Annabelle stood in the silent church sanctuary and breathed in the smell of polished wood and the slight musty aroma from the twenty-year-old hymnals they still used.

She searched for some measure of peace in the quiet solace of her surroundings, but couldn't find it. She guessed she wouldn't find it, either. Maybe never. Steeling herself, she turned to go upstairs to Gregory's office, only he'd come downstairs looking for her.

"Annabelle." He walked over to her and gave her a hug, then pulled back and looked searchingly at her. "What's wrong, sweetheart? Do you have another headache? Can I do something to help?"

She sighed heavily. "Sit down, Gregory. We need to talk."

"I don't understand. Is something wrong?"

Lord, this was going to be harder than she'd thought. She wasn't sure she could get the words out at all. "Gregory, I—I—well, I want you to know that I really thought, I mean I really thought I could do it. But I can't. I just can't."

He took her hand, but she pulled it away. "Don't," she whispered. "Please, don't." She wrapped her hands together in her lap.

"Annabelle, for God's sake, what's wrong?"

There was nothing else to do but blurt it out. "Gregory, I can't see you anymore."

ELEVEN

Gregory looked at her blankly. "I don't understand. What's happened, Annie? What's wrong?"

"I'm sorry, Gregory. So sorry, but the answer is no. I can't marry you."

"What do you mean?" He looked as if he'd been struck, then he closed his eyes for a moment and composed his features. When he spoke, his voice was calm and even. "Why?"

"It wouldn't work. I'm not cut out to be a minister's wife. I'm not the kind of woman who wants to share her husband."

"Does this have anything to do with the times I've run over to Waverly about Fleurique? I told you that Fleurique and the Save the Bay meetings were just short-term things."

"That's not the problem. At least, not all of it."

"Then what is?"

She was going to have to say it, was going to

have to admit her failing. "I can't compete with the biggest rival of all."

"What rival? You're not making any sense."

"Your church. I can't compete with your church. The people here love you, I can see that, and you love them. Your life belongs to them." She blinked back tears. "But I can't compete."

"Annie, I can't give up my church." His words were laced with turmoil.

"No. No, I'm not asking you to. But I can't do this. Somewhere there's a woman who won't mind sharing you and—"

Gregory grabbed her by the shoulders. "Don't you dare tell me I'll find someone else! Do you hear me?" He bit the words out and punctuated them with a little shake. "Don't you dare!"

His tight grip hurt, but Annabelle stood passively in his grasp. She deserved his anger. God only knew, she was angry with herself.

His fingers gentled suddenly. "I don't apologize for who I am, Annie. And I can't promise that I won't get called away time and again, but no one will ever love you more than I will. Please, give me a chance, sweetheart. Give us a chance. We can work this out. I know we can. We love each other."

She walked a few steps away. "Sometimes love just isn't enough. It wasn't enough in college, was it? It didn't save us then." She felt so cold, and she wrapped her arms around herself. She had a gut feeling she might never feel warm again.

"Annie. Tell me what you want me to do, what you need me to say. I'm at a loss."

His voice was tight with pain and it made Annabelle feel even colder. Maybe she'd get so cold that she'd become numb and wouldn't feel the pain anymore. "There's nothing you can do. Gregory, the fault's not with you. You want to change the world and you just might do that one day. On the other hand, I'm happy in my little corner of it."

"Are you? Are you, really?" He sighed, heavily, hopelessly. His eyes were dark and lusterless. "I've fought a lot of fights in my life, but the one thing I can't fight is you. Dammit, Annabelle, I love you. And if that's not enough, I don't know what else I can say."

"I'm sorry." Her words, the barest whisper, floated on the air as she walked away, leaving Gregory gazing after her.

Almost paradise, Gregory thought. He'd had his taste of heaven for about two and a half weeks. Maybe some people never even had that much. And maybe they were the lucky ones because they didn't know the bitterness it left in your soul when it was gone.

Or the hole it left in your gut. A gaping black hole that sucked everything else inside. Joy, happiness, even pain. He felt nothing. Nothing.

Except frustration. What did she want from him? She already had his heart. When they married, she would have had his body. Did she want his soul too? God had laid claim to that years ago.

He closed his eyes and tried praying, but his thoughts were too fragmented. Then the anger began to seep in. He wanted to shout, "Dear God, how could you let me love her only to have it wind up like this?"

He'd have given up every last cause he'd ever fought for if it would have kept her with him, but his ministry wasn't a cause. It was who he was. He could no more give up his ministry than he could give up breathing. But giving up Annabelle was like giving up his heart.

Why did she see his church as her rival? Didn't she think he had love enough to go around? And why couldn't she see she'd be a wonderful preacher's wife? She was so giving and caring and full of love. She would have been terrific working with the kids. She would have been terrific working with anybody.

His head was swimming with thoughts, with pleas, with reasons. And the emotions were suddenly welling up from that emptiness deep inside him. Love, pain, despair, frustration, anger. He wanted to weep, he wanted to shake his fists at heaven, he wanted to grab Annabelle and shake her, he wanted to grab her and kiss her. What he did was shove his fists into his pockets and walk out the church door.

He walked for hours. He walked until even the fireflies had settled down for the night. He walked until he'd narrowed his thoughts to just one thing—putting one foot in front of the other. He wound up in front of Annabelle's again, as if his feet were programmed to end up there. It had to be well past midnight and all the lights were off.

He stood in the street and stared up at the dark windows, feeling as if they were fathomless eyes gazing into his soul and seeing that gut-deep hole that still took up so much space inside. A space filled with loneliness. Strange, he thought, how an empty hole could be filled with loneliness, which was, itself, empty. Emptiness filling emptiness. He slowly turned and headed home, wondering if there was something wrong with him that he couldn't make Annabelle feel loved and needed.

He went to sleep with pain and woke up with pain. It was a heavy leaden weight that he carried with him all day. Somehow, he wasn't sure how, he got through that day and the next and the next. He went by Virgie's to see Annabelle, to try to talk with her, but she'd gone to Raleigh for a few days to help her parents pack for their move to Florida.

Virgie patted his hand sympathetically and told him that maybe all Annabelle needed was a little time to work things through. She'd be back for Daisy's wedding and maybe she'd be more amenable to hearing him out then. That gave him a week to come up with just the right words to say.

She'd never wanted to do anything less in her life. Annabelle stood in a long satin slip in an upstairs room at the church with five giggling half-dressed women. Daisy's sisters were all readying themselves for the wedding. Lily and Rose were fixing their makeup, Caterina was fiddling with her hair, Anne was zipping herself into her frothy pastel bridesmaid's dress. Danni was there, too, fitting her specially tailored dress over her protruding belly.

Annabelle affixed a bright smile on her face and pretended to be interested in what was going on around her. A couple of weeks ago she would have been in the middle of the fun. Now she hung around on the fringes and tried not to spoil anyone else's good time.

Right after Gregory had asked her to marry him, even though she hadn't said yes, she'd allowed herself to dream. To plan. She'd seen herself dressed in white lace, her bridesmaids dressed in aqua chiffon, or maybe rose satin. She'd carried a bouquet of pink roses and baby's breath. Her parents had been there, her father tall and proud, her mother smiling through her tears. Gran had sat in the front row dressed in an apricot-colored suit that complemented her orange hair.

And Gregory. Gregory had been standing by the altar, wearing a boutonniere to match her bouquet. His eyes had lit up when he'd seen her and his smile had glowed with passionate promise.

Gregory would be there today, only instead of

standing beside the bride, he'd be facing the congregation, and the lovely vision in white would be Daisy.

Danni came up beside Annabelle and handed her her dress. "Put this on and I'll zip it up for you."

"I hope you can," Annabelle said morosely. "I've eaten so much fudge-swirl ice cream the past week, I've probably gained ten pounds."

"Maybe, though you look more like you've lost weight to me. Anyway, who's fault is that? To top everything else, you don't look so good. Come over here and let me see what I can do with some concealer and blush. Maybe if we get rid of the circles under your eyes and the pale cheeks, you just might fool everyone into thinking you're fine and dandy." She pushed Annabelle down in a chair and began patting cream beneath her eyes. "Even though you're stubborn, stupid, and bullheaded," she whispered vehemently. "And stop sniffling or we'll have to worry about your red nose too."

"Thanks a lot for your support," Annabelle muttered.

"If I thought you had a grain of sense in your head, you'd have my support hands down. But all I can see is that you're miserable and Gregory's miserable. You walk around looking like a little girl who's lost her teddy bear; he walks around looking like death warmed over. I don't know who's worse, you for starting this whole mess or Gregory for letting you get away with it."

Caterina glanced in their direction and both Danni and Annabelle smiled for her benefit. "I did what I had to do," Annabelle said to Danni in a low voice. "Can you see me being a preacher's wife? Can you see me losing my husband to choir practice on Wednesdays, visitations, funerals, weddings? Losing my husband to everyone else in town? Knowing that everyone else will always be more important than I am?"

"You idiot! Not more important, just more urgent at the time. And yes, since you asked, I *can* see you being a preacher's wife. If you had any sense—" Danni broke off when Daisy entered the room in a flurry of tulle and white chiffon.

Annabelle's throat tightened and her eyes filled with tears. Daisy looked beautiful, and Annabelle wished more than anything in the world that that lovely glowing woman with roses in her hair and yards of tulle veiling could be herself.

All the bridesmaids crowded around, each giving Daisy a small gift. Anne gave her a gold bracelet she'd found in an antique shop. Lily gave her a charm to attach to the bracelet. Rose lent Daisy her pearl earrings, Caterina gave her a blue satin garter. Danni and Annabelle had a real English sixpence to put in her shoe, though how she'd secure it in her open-toed sandals was anyone's guess.

Annabelle heard the first strains of the processional and knew the mothers of the bride and groom were being seated. This was their cue to go downstairs. Taking a deep breath, she followed the others down, with Daisy bringing up the rear.

As they stood in the vestibule waiting for Emmy Tanner, the flower girl, to finish distributing her basket of rose petals, Annabelle peeked around the door and saw Buddy and his brother, Jimmy, waiting at the front of the church. Then she saw Gregory and her heart pounded. He was wearing his ministerial robes and standing next to Buddy, looking so official.

Annabelle hoped she'd be able to steel her legs enough to get her down the aisle. Somehow, she hadn't thought about how difficult it would be to walk down the church aisle dressed in a chiffon dress, with Gregory waiting at the end. To marry another couple.

He hadn't seen Annabelle yet. But here came Anne, dressed in mint-green chiffon, followed by Caterina in peach, Rose in blue, Lily in lilac, Danni in pink. He saw Magda's hand in all this. She'd often said the Gypsy side of her knew what color someone should wear, and she'd apparently dressed each bridesmaid in what she saw as the appropriate color. Then he saw Annabelle.

Gregory's breath caught in his throat and his fingers clenched around the book he held. She wore a pale gold dress that picked up the gold streaks in her beautiful hair. But she should have been wearing white. And she should have been wearing a soft intimate smile just for him and not that bright fake thing she'd stuck on. Her gaze should have been rich with promise and locked on his, not skittering around looking everywhere but at him.

He closed his eyes against a fresh surge of pain and clenched his jaw with resolve. After this wedding was over, he and Annabelle were going to settle things once and for all. He opened his book, smiled at Daisy and Buddy, and began the service.

He managed to keep his attention on the ceremony, except when Danni and Sebastian's cat strolled down the center aisle as casually as if he'd been invited and sat down next to Sebastian. His mouth twitched at Sebastian's grimace and he glanced at Annabelle only to find her looking at him. They smiled together in a brief moment of shared amusement, then Annabelle's smile faded and she looked away.

With an effort, Gregory turned his attention back to the wedding ceremony. "Do you, Daisy, take this man to be your lawful wedded husband?"

Daisy stood silent for so long, a murmur began to rise from the congregation. Finally she sighed and kissed Buddy on the cheek. "Sorry, Buddy, but I think this is best. No, Reverend, I don't." With that, she handed her bouquet to Caterina, tossed her yards of tulle veiling over one arm, and turned to walk down the aisle.

Buddy gave a philosophical shrug and faced the congregation. "Well, I don't think there's going to be a wedding after all. But feel free to attend the reception on the church lawn. Lots of good food." With that, he followed his ex-bride down the aisle and out the door.

After a moment of stunned silence, everyone began talking. All of Daisy's sisters hurried after her to find out what was going on while kids ran out the door to be first in line at the reception tables. Elsie Wilson began to hyperventilate and had to be laid down on a pew with Bosco frantically fanning her.

Gregory knew he should stay and try to calm Elsie, or find Daisy or Buddy and see if they needed his help, but when he saw Annabelle trying to slip out the side door, he went after her instead. He grabbed her arm and said, "I'll give you a ride."

"I can wait for Danni."

"I'll give you a ride." He called to Danni, "I'm taking Annabelle," and pulled her out the door.

Annabelle couldn't get away without making a scene, and two minutes later she found herself in the front seat of Gregory's Mustang. "Don't you need to do something about that mess inside?" she asked him.

"Bosco's looking after Elsie. Daisy's a grown woman and has already made her decision, and Buddy didn't look any too crushed, if you noticed." Gregory started the car and pulled out of the church parking lot. "Everybody's taken care of, except you and me. We've got some unfinished business to discuss."

"Gregory, we said everything that needed to be said."

Gregory never took his eyes off the road, but his jaw tightened. "If I'm not mistaken, *you* said everything you needed to say. I didn't have much of a chance. I want my chance now. You owe me."

"Rehashing everything isn't going to make any difference."

"I don't intend to rehash anything. I intend to set you straight on a few misconceptions. The first being—"

"What's that?" she interrupted.

"What's what?"

She pointed to an orange glow in the night sky. "That."

"Oh God," Gregory muttered. "I hope that's not what I think it is." As he drove closer it became apparent that the orange glow was a house fire. "It's the McKinleys'." He parked the car as close as he could without getting in the way of the fire engines, and he and Annabelle walked the block to the house.

Gregory immediately went over to the man and woman standing in the street watching their house blaze and arguing with each other. Annabelle stared in horrified fascination as the flames flared up, as if trying to reach the sky with their searing touch. And then she noticed the three children huddled together in a little group. They were, she guessed, between the ages of six and ten, and she recognized the oldest, Seth, from the church play.

She walked over to them oblivious to her chiffon dress, and squatted down. "Hi, Seth. Is this your brother and sister?" The child gave a solemn nod, and she said, "Why don't you come over here with me, out of the firemen's way, and we'll sit in the grass?"

Annabelle pulled out every last tidbit she'd ever learned about child psychology and managed to get the kids' attention focused, at least a little, on her.

The fire was put out quickly, and Annabelle went over to hear what the fire chief had to tell the McKinleys. Her eyes locked with Gregory's for a telling moment, then she returned to assure the kids that the kitchen had sustained most of the damage. Their clothes would all need to be washed but would be okay, as well as their toys and bedroom furniture. Once they'd been reassured, they willingly listened to her tell stories. The little girl, Gloria, was starting to yawn and rub her eyes already, the excitement and terror taking its toll.

After a while Gregory came over and sat next to the kids. He had a quiet word for each of them and said a simple prayer that seemed to reassure them. Turning to Annabelle, he ran his fingers over her face, wiping at a sooty smudge on her cheek. "Thank you," he said so softly only she could hear.

"All I've done is tell them a few stories."

"And reassure them and make them feel safe and secure. And give them some special attention at a time when they're scared and confused."

She smiled. "Isn't that about what you've done with their parents?"

He smiled back. "I don't know how much longer I'll be. Do you want me to run you home?"

"I'm okay here. I'll wait for you." She turned back to the children and told another story. Before long, the two youngest had snuggled close to her and dozed off, while Seth huddled down with his arms around his dog.

Seth finally dozed off, too, and Annabelle sat there in the grass and watched as the firemen walked through the house one more time to make sure everything was okay. It was late, the air was cool, and she felt a strange peace settle over her. She had felt needed tonight. Maybe she'd made a difficult time for those kids just a little easier by being there.

She chewed on her lip and thought about that some more while she absently watched Gregory help the McKinleys make arrangements for a place to stay for the next few days. It occurred to her that he must feel the same sense of satisfaction when he'd made a difference in someone's life. Even if it was just for a few minutes.

This was why she'd wanted to teach. To make that difference, particularly in the lives of children.

Had she not given Gregory credit for wanting to do the same thing?

"You ready to go?" he asked her, holding out a hand to help her to her feet.

She nodded and smiled, taking his hand. The ride to her grandmother's was quiet, but not uncomfortably so. It was, instead, a thoughtful quiet.

When Gregory stopped the car in front of Virgie's, he turned to her. "It's late, but we still need to talk." His gaze, dark and unreadable, lingered on her face.

"I know," she said. "And I think maybe we should. Tomorrow?"

He seemed surprised at her easy acquiescence. "Uh, yeah. Tomorrow. Or later today, as the case may be."

"Later today. If it won't interfere with your Saturday sermon writing."

"I don't have to write one this week. It's youth Sunday. They've taken over the service for the day. I get to be just an ordinary guy for a change. Do you, uh, want to call me when you wake up? I expect I'll be around the house most of the day."

"I'll call you, then." She let herself out of the car, then bent down. "Lock your door, Rev," she admonished lightly, and walked up the sidewalk and went inside.

Gregory sat and watched until he saw the light go on in her bedroom. Whatever reaction he'd been expecting from her, this wasn't it.

He shook his head and started his car. He

wasn't going to complain. At least the loneliness inside him had receded a little.

Annabelle lay on her side petting the cat who'd appeared in her bedroom after she'd lain awake for an hour or so. This inability to sleep was getting to be the norm as far as Gregory was concerned. She really needed to think about some things and had hoped to do it after a good night's sleep.

No such luck. Her brain wouldn't shut off. Neither would her heart. There seemed to be some master plan, some incredible bit of wisdom that lay just out of her grasp. It was as if she could almost touch it, almost see it, but not quite. Somehow she knew that if she figured that one thing out, everything else would fall into place. Tonight, with Gregory, it had seemed close indeed.

Maybe if she talked to him, she could figure it out. She sat up and reached for the phone. No, she didn't want a telephone line between them. She wanted to see his face, watch his eyes. Perhaps that would help her find the answer. She just wished she was sure what the question was.

She quickly dressed and left a note on her bedroom door, in case her grandmother woke up and looked for her. She didn't allow herself time to think as she drove to Gregory's; she was afraid she'd change her mind. She thanked God that his light was still on, because she might not have had enough nerve to knock on the door if he'd already gone to bed.

He opened the door almost immediately. "Annabelle."

"Hi." Oh Lord, he was wearing jeans and nothing else. For a moment Annabelle forgot what she wanted to say.

"Is something wrong? Is Virgie all right?"

She took a deep breath and willed her gaze not to stray below his chin. "Nothing's wrong and Gran's fine. I just, well, I couldn't sleep and I thought maybe we could talk."

He smiled faintly and invited her in, waving his hand at the sofa. "I couldn't sleep either. Sit. Do you, uh, can I get you something?"

She shook her head. "No thanks." She fell silent. He was the one who'd wanted to talk earlier, and she hoped he'd start things. He didn't. "Gregory, you said I had a couple of—of—"

"Misconceptions."

"Yeah, misconceptions you wanted to correct. What did you mean?" She looked at him, her gaze locking with his, and she wondered if this was indeed where the answer was.

He sat silent for a long moment, as if gathering his words carefully. "The biggest one is that you seem to think I'm looking for you to be a *part* of my life. I'm not. I'm looking for you to *share* my life. Everything I'm a part of, you'd be a part of. I want a partner, Annie. A real honest-to-God partner."

She could hear the underlying tension in his voice and she could tell that what he was saying was important to him. Studying him, she saw the quiet longing in his eyes, the fervent hope that he'd somehow get through to her. Tears stung her own eyes, and she wanted to tell him that she was listening, really listening, to him. With her heart.

He reached out as if to take her hand, then pulled back. "You were right, you know, when you said the ministry is my life. It is. But it doesn't have to be something I do while you do your thing over there somewhere. It's something we do together, Annie.

"Do you remember I said that our goals weren't so different? I wanted to save souls and you wanted to save minds."

She nodded. "I remember."

"Well, the two aren't exclusive of each other. We can do both."

"I kept watching you with the McKinleys," she said. "You were so good with them. I couldn't hear what you were saying, but whatever it was, it seemed to help because they hugged each other and they smiled at you. You made a real difference to them, just like you did with Mrs. Cochran's family at the hospital."

"You were good with the kids. You made a real difference with them too. Don't you see, Annie? We could work together. We could work to make this whole community a better place. We could work to make a marriage work, to build a home together."

He reached out again to take her hand, this time holding it in both of his. "I don't just want to come home *to* you, Annie, I want to walk in that door *with* you."

This was it, she thought. This was that home truth, that pearl of wisdom she'd been reaching for. It was that word. *With*. Her throat was suddenly so tight, she had trouble getting the words out, but she gave a shaky smile. "I can't do choir. I sing like a frog, remember?"

An answering smile, a tender smile, crossed his face. "I remember. If I sing like a cricket, we'll sound like a summer night."

Hope blossomed inside her like a rose. "Do you really think we can do it?" she asked tremulously.

"Sweetheart, I think we can do anything if we work on it together. We can do miracles. I love you, Annie. I love you so much. I'll try as hard as I can to make sure you always feel loved, to make sure you never feel left out. But I need you in my life. Please, Annie, tell me what I need to do."

The tears overflowed at his heartfelt plea and ran freely down her cheeks. She whispered, "Well, you might ask me to marry you again."

He clasped her hand so hard, it should have hurt, only she didn't feel any pain. The welling of joy inside her eclipsed everything else but the glimmer of tears in his eyes.

"Will you marry me, Annie?"

"Yes."

She was pulled into his arms so fast, she didn't have time to breathe. Not that it mattered, because his mouth crushed hers, stealing what little breath she had left anyway. And, in a moment, she really didn't care all that much about breathing. She had not only found her master plan, her home truth, but she was wrapped tightly in it. Surrounded by it. It was his arms.

EPILOGUE

"You can't come in, Gregory. You're not supposed to see the bride before the wedding."

"I know, I know. I just want to talk to her a minute. Please, Danni."

Danni sighed. "Fine, but don't you come in. Understand? You don't even peek around the door."

"I wouldn't dream of it. You might sit on me if I disobeyed you. Sebastian says that's how you keep him in line these days."

"Don't you forget it. Hey, Annabelle, there's a gentleman at the door who insists on talking to you. Make it quick. Your groom-to-be should be heading downstairs about now. You can crack the door to talk to him, but don't let him see you."

Annabelle went over to the door, wrapping her fingers around the edge of it. "Gregory?"

He covered her fingers with his. "I love you, sweetheart. I just wanted to tell you."

Annabelle's smile, which she'd walked around with all morning, grew wider. "You can prove it by meeting me downstairs in about five minutes. And, by the way, I love you too."

"You can prove it by accepting a present I have for you. I've had it for nine years and I really want you to have it."

"Okay. I can't wait to see it."

His other hand showed around the door, holding his college ring. "Will you be my girl?"

Annabelle took the ring from him and bent to press a kiss on his fingers. "Yes. I'll see you in five."

Gran, dressed in a lemon-yellow dress that blended nicely with her newly dyed blond hair, gave Annabelle a quick hug and went downstairs. Her mother, weepy but overjoyed, kissed Annabelle and hurried after Gran, and her father offered his arm with the aplomb of a prince. Danni, looking for all the world like a pink chiffon balloon, led the way.

Annabelle stood in the vestibule at the back of the church, holding the college ring she'd slipped on the gold chain around her neck, and peeked up at the front. Her parents' minister from Raleigh, here to perform the ceremony, stared down at the cat sitting on the floor next to his feet. Gregory and Sebastian stood to one side waiting, with Gregory wearing a boutonniere of pink rosebuds and baby's breath—to match her bouquet. His eyes eagerly searched the back of the church for a glimpse of his bride.

And then it was time. Annabelle thought she'd never forget this beautiful September day as long as she lived. The afternoon sun streamed in the windows, casting a golden glow on everything. Or maybe it was just that her eyes were seeing gold. Then the only thing she was seeing was Gregory's face and his beautiful, beautiful eyes.

"Dearly beloved . . ."

Annabelle heard the words through a mist, her only reality Gregory's strong hands, which held hers so firmly, his golden-brown eyes so full of love and sweet desire that she wanted to drown in them. "And now by the power vested in me—"

"Damn!"

That wasn't part of the wedding ceremony. Annabelle jerked her head around and looked at Danni.

Danni gave an apologetic shrug. "My water just broke."

The best man's knees buckled.

And Annabelle and Gregory spent their anxiously and long-awaited wedding night in a hospital waiting room.

It was dawn before they arrived at Gregory's house. Gregory swung Annabelle into his arms and carried her across the threshold. He carried her straight to his bed, quickly undressed her to bra and panties, leaving the white lacy gown lying on the floor topped with his discarded tuxedo. He lay next to her on the bed, pulling her into his arms, then kissed her, a singularly sweet kiss. He pulled back enough to see her face. "I love you, Mrs. Talbott." He kissed her nose. "Go to sleep, sweetheart."

"Gregory?"

He grinned, a tired but purely male grin. "Neither of us has slept in over twenty-four hours and when I make love with you, I want you to be wellrested. You're going to need to be."

Annabelle smiled sleepily. "And you're definitely going to need to be well-rested, too, my love."

He snuggled Annabelle next to him and rested his cheek on top of her head. "I intend to be," he whispered, but her lashes had already drifted shut.

When Gregory awoke, long fingers of golden afternoon reached across the bed. "God, I could wake up like this everyday for the rest of my life," he whispered as he snuggled his new bride closer.

She stirred and opened her eyes. "So could I," she murmured sleepily, and stretched, which brought even more of her body in contact with his.

He raised up on one arm and leaned over her. "Good afternoon, sweetheart," he said, pressing soft moist kisses on her nose, her forehead, her eyelids, her chin. He kissed one corner of her mouth, then the other, then left a trail of kisses down her cheek. Only when Annabelle's fingers curled imperiously into his hair and met his lips with hers, did he take her mouth.

"I love your mouth," he murmured against her lips. "I love the way it fits against mine. I love the way you taste. I could kiss you for hours." And then he kissed her, long drugging kisses that gave credence to his words.

When he finally lifted his head, he deftly unfastened her bra and tossed it aside. "But I love your breasts, too," he whispered huskily. "I love the way they fit my hands. I love the way they taste." He suited actions to words until her breasts swelled into his palms and her nipples beaded tightly in his mouth.

Annabelle moaned again and again beneath his skilled touches, soft pleading sounds, primal animal sounds. Her hands roamed the warm skin of his back, sweeping over the smooth ripples of his muscles again and again.

Gregory raised up long enough to remove her silky panties, then his own, then pressed kisses down over her flat stomach. "And I love you here, too. So hot and wet—" His voice broke off as his lips found her. He loved her with lips and hands until she shook with pleasure. He loved her until she wound her hands in his hair and pulled his face up to hers for a thorough kiss.

"I thought marriage was supposed to be a fifty-fifty deal," she complained breathlessly though with an infinitely satisfied smile.

Gregory's brow creased a little. "Of course it is, sweetheart."

"So when do I get my fifty percent?" Annabelle punctuated her words with a sweep of her fingertips down his back and up again.

In sudden comprehension, Gregory rolled over on his back and sighed, a long-suffering sigh, belied by his muscles, tensed with anticipation. "Oh well, if I must. Go ahead and do your worst. I can take it."

"You think so?" Annabelle's hair fell forward and brushed over his chest as she brushed her lips over the dusting of soft red-gold curls in the center. She circled his flat nipples with her tongue, then nipped the tiny buds with her teeth. "I think I'll have you begging for mercy in no time."

"You may be right." Gregory tried to catch his breath as his fingers tangled restlessly in her hair.

Annabelle let her long-denied hunger take over and she tasted and teased until Gregory cried out, "You win. Have mercy!" and rolled over, pinning her beneath him.

He caught his breath as he looked down at her, her hair spread over his pillow, her eyes glowing with love, her face flushed with desire. "I love you, sweetheart," he breathed as he slowly entered her, and the words were as heartfelt and sacred as a prayer.

"And I love you," she whispered back, as she held him tightly in her arms.

"It's so good. It's so good," he said hoarsely as

he buried his face in her hair. "I've needed you, only you, for so long."

"I've needed you all my life," Annabelle said and those were the last rational words either of them spoke for some time, though the silence was broken with incoherent murmurs of love and need.

Gregory made love to her with his heart as well as his body and when she finally cried out with ecstasy, he answered those cries with his own muffled shouts of possession and triumph.

Gregory felt gloriously wasted as he lay with Annabelle's head cradled on his shoulder. Her fingers smoothed back and forth over his chest, her leg nestled between his. When he heard her giggle a little, he snuggled her closer. "What's so funny?" he asked.

She sighed, a sweet floaty sound of pure joy. "I was just thinking that all things come to those who wait. But last night I wasn't so sure about this waiting business."

He grinned and kissed the top of her head, his free hand tracing little circles between her breasts. "We should have known Danni would go into labor, even if it was a month early. Babies keep their own timetables, I hear. Especially twins. I wonder how Sebastian is going to take to having two more little pink-and-purple butterflies flitting around."

"He was absolutely thrilled about having girls. How about you? Boys or girls?"

"I'd be thrilled with either one. As long as their mother is you." He turned onto his side to kiss her, leaving a moist trail from her lips down to her breasts.

She arched under his touch and breathed, "Suppose a minister turned out to have a wife with an insatiable appetite for his body?"

"Then he's particularly blessed, sweetheart," Gregory said, groaning as she reciprocated his caresses. "Blessed, indeed."

THE EDITORS' CORNER

If it's love you're looking for, you've come to the right place. Our TREASURED TALES IV romances brim with excitement and adventure as your favorite authors add a sexy contemporary spin to everyone's favorite classics. Each of these wonderful novels features memorable characters finding love in the unlikeliest of places. TREASURED TALES IV is your invitation to join them on the most romantic journey of all.

Goldilocks is more than a match for three big, bad bears in Debra Dixon's **BAD TO THE BONE, LOVESWEPT #774.** He's a brand of danger she's never risked, with the most unforgiving pair of blue eyes that ever stared into her troubled soul, yet Jessica Daniels insists she doesn't have the answers to Detective Sullivan Kincaid's questions about a missing person. But the innocent act doesn't fit with the way the mysterious brunette arouses Sully's suspicions—and his most forbidden desires. Debra Dixon delivers a once-in-a-lifetime read with this powerfully emotional, savagely sensual, yet utterly romantic novel.

Romance Writers of America president Janis Reams Hudson delights with **ANGEL ON A HARLEY,** LOVESWEPT #775. Just as Whitney Houston confounds Kevin Costner in the instant classic movie THE BODYGUARD, Faith Hillman isn't at all what Dalton McShane expects when he faces the woman who claims she is carrying his child. And Dalton McShane isn't what she's been expecting either. Right name, wrong guy . . . Clearly, Faith is a woman betrayed—big time. Then, an act of violence makes it obvious that if ever there is a woman in need of a knight in shining armor, Faith is it. Weaving a story of forbidden passion and potent seduction, of unspoken dreams and second chances, Janis Reams Hudson celebrates the sweet power of enduring love and its healing magic.

MIDNIGHT HEAT, LOVESWEPT #776, is the provocative finale to Donna Kauffman's THE THREE MUSKETEERS trilogy. They call him The Predator, the investigator who never leaves a case unsolved, and now Dane Colbourne has set his sights on her! Adria Burke knows her quick response prevented a tragic midair collision, but Dane wants evidence that proves her case—and his fierce, hot look tells her he wants her just as much. When men who'll risk anything finally taste irresistible danger in the arms of women who can't help getting a little too close to the flame, there's no one better to write their stories than Donna Kauffman.

Last but by no means least, Faye Hughes shines

with star power in **WILD AT HEART,** LOVE-SWEPT #777, inspired by the timelessly appealing movie IT HAPPENED ONE NIGHT. In Faye's delicious homage, Jake Wilder crashes a party looking for scandal and maybe a chance at redemption, but when Maggie Thorpe drags him into a closet to elude his pursuers, what else could he do but kiss her breathless? Her untamed heart recognizes a kindred spirit beneath Jake's outrageous charm, but once they team up to expose a shady deal, the sinfully sexy reporter must convince the rebel heiress they are meant to be partners in passion forever. Sparkling with wicked fun and seductive as a Southern drawl from a bad boy's lips, this tantalizing tale of love in close quarters shows just why Faye Hughes is a fan favorite every time!

Happy reading!

With warmest wishes,

Beth de Guzman

Shauna Summers

Beth de Guzman   Shauna Summers
Senior Editor   Associate Editor

P.S. Watch for these Bantam women's fiction titles coming in February: *New York Times* bestselling au-

Don't miss these extraordinary books
by your favorite Bantam authors

On sale in December:

BREAKFAST IN BED
by Sandra Brown

NIGHT SINS
by Tami Hoag

VANITY
by Jane Feather

DEATH ELIGIBLE
by Judith Henry Wall

SAXON BRIDE
by Tamara Leigh

Her novels are sensual and moving, compelling and richly satisfying. That's why Sandra Brown is one of America's best-loved romance writers. Now, the New York Times *bestselling author of* HEAVEN'S PRICE *captures the wrenching dilemma of a woman tempted by an unexpected —and forbidden—love.*

BREAKFAST IN BED
by Sandra Brown

"No one understands sexual fantasy better than Sandra Brown. . . . Ms. Brown inventively blends a variety of fantasies into the fabric of her very real romance."
—*Romantic Times*

Erotic, touching, and true, BREAKFAST IN BED *is one of Sandra Brown's classic romances available in hardcover for the first time.*

VANITY
by Jane Feather

*From romance's newest rising star comes a new triumph of
romance. Brimming with passionate emotion and compelling adventure, here is Jane Feather at her most unforget-
table.*

"I presume you too have a name, sir," she said in an
attempt to recapture her earlier assurance.

"Oh, most certainly," he agreed, taking a ja-
panned snuffbox from the deep pocket of his coat. He
flicked the lid and delicately took a pinch.

Nothing else was forthcoming. Octavia tapped her
foot on the stone lintel. "Am I to be told it, sir?"

He looked at her, one eyebrow quizzically raised.
"I confess I hadn't given the question any thought.
However . . ." He bowed, managing an elegant
flourish in the confined space. "At this moment Lord
Nick is at your service, Miss Morgan."

She stared at him, trying to remember where
she'd heard the name before. And what did he mean
by *at this moment*? "Oh?" she said, her jaw dropping.
"Lord Nick, the highwayman?"

He smiled and shrugged. "Such calumny. I don't
know where people get these stories from."

Octavia shook her head as if trying to clear her
thoughts. No gentleman, after all, but Lord Nick, the

highwayman given the devil's colloquial name for his uncanny ability to evade the law. If he was who he said he was—not that he looked in the least as she'd imagined a highwayman would look—then it seemed unlikely he was intending to lay a charge against her. But it seemed only reasonable and friendly in the circumstances to return his property without further delay. She slipped her hand inside her cloak, sliding her fingers into the slit in her gown, intending to extract the watch from the pouch. Then she realized that he was watching her every movement, a sardonic spark in his eyes.

She let her hand fall to her side and smiled nonchalantly. She didn't like the look in those slate-gray eyes, and this was far too public a spot for an unsolicited admission of guilt, even to a fellow pirate.

The rushing mob was diminishing now, the cries and screams fading into the distance.

"Come," Lord Nick said. "I think it's safe to leave now."

"You go your way and I'll go mine, sir," she said, stepping out of the doorway. There was no sign now of a sedan chair; the chairmen would have made off to safety as soon as the cry of "press gang" had gone up —they were strong, well-muscled men, perfect candidates for His Majesty's Navy.

"You seem remarkably obtuse for someone who I'm convinced has a sharp head on her shoulders," her companion remarked in a tone of mild exasperation. "We have yet to have our little discussion, if you recall." He looked round, getting his bearings. "My horse is at the Rose and Crown . . . this way, I believe."

"I'm not coming with you," Octavia said quietly, her anger visible only in her snapping eyes and her increased pallor. "I don't know what you have in mind, but if you attempt to abduct me, I'll scream so loudly it'll bring every constable in the area."

He appeared not to have heard her, his attention directed toward the lad bringing his horse, a big-shouldered roan who looked easily capable of carrying two riders.

"Now, Miss Morgan . . . pillion or in front of me?" He turned back to her. "Either will be perfectly comfortable, I assure you. Peter is as steady as a rock."

"Are you perhaps hard of hearing?" Octavia asked, her voice low and fierce. "I bid you good day." She spun on her heel and stalked out of the yard, her back prickling as she waited for the arresting hand on her shoulder. But nothing happened. She walked unmolested out of the yard of the Rose and Crown and into the narrow cobbled lane.

The pounding of hooves behind her at first didn't intrude on her reverie. When they did, they were almost upon her. She was hurrying down the center of the lane, avoiding the filthy water and refuse in the kennel at the side. Now she had no choice but to jump sideways, splashing through the kennel, if she wasn't to be run down. It was a common enough hazard in the side streets of the city.

"A pox on your knavish soul!" she swore in most unladylike accents as the kennel filth caked her boots and soiled the hem of her cloak and gown that she hadn't had time to lift clear. "May you rot in . . ."

The rest of the curse was lost as the rider drew

abreast of her, swooped low in the saddle, and caught her up with all the dexterity of a performer at Philip Astley's Amphitheatre.

Octavia found herself in the saddle of the roan, the hard body of Lord Nick at her back, his encircling arm holding her steady on her perch.

She opened her mouth and screamed, a shrill, piercing clamor. Casements were flung open along the lane, curious faces hanging out, peering down through the thickening veil of snow.

"You wish to visit the local magistrate?" Lord Nick murmured against her ear, making no attempt to still her screams. "I'm sure he'll be interested in what you're concealing beneath your skirt."

"Let me down and I'll give you back your god-damned watch!" Octavia exclaimed.

"Oh, yes, you will give it back to me," he agreed equably. "All in good time, though, Miss Morgan. All in good time."

DEATH ELIGIBLE

by the bestselling author of
MOTHER LOVE

Judith Henry Wall

A family is held together by bonds stronger than the law. But what happens when that family must make a choice to give up one of its own? Could they sacrifice their own mentally handicapped son to save the life of one of his siblings? In this mesmerizing new novel, Judith Henry Wall asks this provocative question as she plumbs the depths of one family's secret heart.

The police had come just as they were sitting down to dinner—to arrest him for murder. Hours later, Maura cleared away the uneaten meal, stopping every few minutes to wipe her eyes with her apron.

Angie took a sip of water to help the cracker go down and took another from the package.

Had the rest of the household been able to sleep, she wondered, or had they, like her, in spite of bourbon and sleeping pills, replayed the horrible scenario of Danny's being arrested over and over? And the ten o'clock news. Danny being dragged into the city jail.

She'd been sitting here at this same table on the morning of her twenty-first birthday, when her parents asked if they could name her Danny's guardian in their wills—darling Danny, who was even then taller than Angie but would remain forever a child.

Angie was surprised that her parents felt the need

to ask. She'd always assumed that she eventually would be the family member to assume responsibility for Danny. But assumptions weren't enough for her parents. They needed a formal commitment from her. They wanted her to look them in the eye and say yes, she would be Danny's guardian after they were gone.

Angie had come around the table to kneel between her parents, to put her arms around them and say, of course, she would look after Danny. Always.

She accepted responsibility for him even though being his guardian would limit her options and complicate her life. But she loved him too much not to. Her love for him was unconditional. Even maternal.

Angie pushed the package of crackers away and took another sip of water. All about her, the house was heavy with silence.

She'd told the arresting officers not to handcuff Danny. He couldn't stand to be restrained. And he was so strong. He used a shoulder to slam one officer against the wall and his head to knock the other one off his feet. One of them had actually reached for his handgun when her father's voice suddenly resounded through the entry hall. "Get out of here—both of you. I'll take my son to jail myself."

"I'm sorry, Judge Tarrington, but you know we can't do that," the older detective explained.

"The hell you can't," he'd said, pointing to the door. "I will call the mayor, the police commissioner, the governor, the president, and God himself if you don't take off those damned handcuffs and get out of here!"

But Danny would have it all to go through again

Monday morning when they handcuffed him and dragged him into a courtroom, where he'd be asked how he pled—guilty or not guilty of killing Beth Williams.

Angie tried to think—did Danny even know what the word "guilty" meant?

"Oh, God," she said out loud.

At first, after he didn't die of the encephalitis that left him mentally impaired, he'd been a happy little soul, unless he thought someone was mad at him. Then he would cry. Even when he was a pest, they were seldom mean to him. Except Matt. Matt had little patience with his retarded twin.

But after the kidnaping, Danny came home a changed boy. He screamed if startled. His feelings were easily hurt. He had nightmares. He got hysterical if restrained. A mama cat got upset with his handling of her babies and scratched his hand. Danny stomped on the cat and killed it. And he beat up Manuel's son after he jumped out from behind a bush and said "boo"—really beat him, breaking his nose and collarbone.

Beth came to live in the room next to Danny's after the kidnaping—after it was decided to keep Danny at home, where he would be safe, where no strange woman would walk onto the school playground and take him away.

When Beth first came to them, she was twenty years old, a special-education major at UT-Arlington. Frank had been eighteen, Angie fifteen, Julia twelve, Danny and Matt almost eight. Their parents had called everyone into the living room to meet her. Beth, wearing a crisp white blouse and a navy skirt, was standing in front of the high arched window, her mass of hair a halo of golden red in the sunlight.

After Beth came, Danny did better, even started singing again. Beth taught Danny to count and write his name. She taught him to swim and when it was all right to laugh and sing and when he was supposed to be a very quiet boy. She encouraged him to run sprints, timing him, training him, teaching him technique. When he was the first runner across the finish line in the 100-yard-dash finals of the 1980 Special Olympics, the whole family cheered and wept with the joy of it. It was a miracle. And they had Beth to thank for it.

But Danny never completely lost the dark side that he brought home from the kidnaping. His nightmares became occasional, but when he had them, they were terrible. And what had previously manifested itself as frustration when he couldn't work a puzzle or color inside the lines would sometimes cause him to dissolve into bouts of uncontrollable crying. The whole family learned to intercede when tears threatened, to redirect his attention to some other activity. It hurt too much to see Danny cry. Sometimes all that was required was to hug him, even after he was no longer a little boy, even when physically he was the largest member of the family, larger even than his twin brother. Danny needed lots of hugs. Because of him, they were a family of huggers.

Looking back, Angie often wondered if the kidnapers hadn't meant to take Matt, the normal twin. Those outside the family always seemed to regard Danny as some sort of stepchild or charity case and not a true Tarrington.

But Danny made them special and defined them as a family. He taught them tolerance and patience. He shared his wonder at the world with them—and his innocence, even after he was grown, with whiskers on his chin and a disturbing fascination for anything female.

Beth didn't have a family. Angie couldn't imagine such a thing. With three brothers and a sister, she had always been surrounded by family. Her Tarrington grandparents lived behind them, just the other side of the back gate. And her family visited frequently with her mother's parents, who had retired in Austin.

Angie and her little sister, Julia, decided right away that Beth was to be part of their family. Their big sister. And it did seem that way sometimes. But they were born Tarringtons, and Beth only worked for their family. She wanted it, though—to be a Tarrington. None of them realized how much.

SAXON BRIDE

by the author of
PAGAN BRIDE

Tamara Leigh

Once Maxen Pendery was a man of God. Then he was told that his brother had been murdered by a Saxon wench, and he knew he could not rest until he took revenge. Yet when he finally captured Rhiannyn of Etheverry, something unexpected stirred within him. True, she was breathtakingly lovely; but never once did she use her woman's wiles to battle him, only her sharp tongue and strong will . . . leaving Maxen torn between his duty and an agonizing truth: he would do anything to conquer this golden-haired maid, even if the price was his very soul.

Maxen, now Brother Justus to the Saxons, watched Rhiannyn cross the glade behind Edwin. At first sight he had been uncertain she was the same woman who had spent so many weeks in the castle dungeons, for her resemblance to that creature was distant.

But it was she, and even more lovely than he'd imagined she would be beneath the dirt, grime, and bruises. Hair that had only whispered of gold now gleamed that color, the cream of her skin was accented by the tint of roses in each cheek, and a shape that had promised much beneath her tattered bliaut had more than fulfilled its promise in the belted tunic and hose she wore to practice her swordskill. She was beautiful, almost angelic, and more than capable of luring spellbound men to their death.

Aye, it was Rhiannyn of Etheverry, though stronger than before. Maxen had felt her resolve, seen it in her eyes, her carriage, and her stiffening back when Edwin had called her to task. A small woman with the strength of many.

But he would break her, Maxen vowed, his resentment over the hold she had on him lending him determination. Then the woman who was a scourge to the vows of his body—vows she had forced him to renounce—would be forever exorcised.

As the man called Aethel came toward him, Maxen glanced one last time at Rhiannyn. Positioned before the pel, she assumed the proper stance and angled her sword in readiness for a mock attack. Though she did not look to Edwin, he spoke to her, gestured, then stepped back.

As Maxen had wondered whether Thomas had lain with Rhiannyn, he now wondered the same about Edwin, but then Rhiannyn dealt the wooden post an admirable blow and sped his thoughts elsewhere. He frowned. Perhaps she had spoken true, he reflected. Mayhap it was she who had murdered Thomas after all. Though he thought it, he still was not convinced. It had to be another.

With that in mind, Maxen swept his searching gaze over those who had returned to their intense training and, surprisingly, found that many appeared quite worthy. Their swings strong, their aim sure, they promised a well-matched battle when next they set themselves upon the castle to take back what they claimed was theirs. And it was theirs, a vexatious voice reminded him.

Had been theirs, he countered, but no more. Regardless, he must not forget his reason for coming into Edwin's grim world.

Though Maxen had experienced doubt when he'd listened in on Rhiannyn's conversation with Christophe and heard her tell him that it was not Edwin who had killed Thomas, he had only believed it after following her to this place and seeing the injury to the man's fighting arm. As Rhiannyn had said, it would have been impossible for him to have thrown the dagger after receiving such a serious wound. Assuredly, it had not been Edwin; but who then? Which one of these men had plunged his dagger into Thomas's heart and bled his life upon that field?

A fire growing in him, Maxen lowered his gaze so the great, hulking Aethel would not see the betraying depths of his eyes.

Aye, he told himself in an attempt to calm his blood, soon every last one of Edwin's rebels would know the yoke of Norman rule, including Rhiannyn. First, though, he must discover who had murdered Thomas and insure that the villain did not simply die but that he suffered as Thomas had.

To enter the sweepstakes outlined below, you must respond by the date specified and follow all entry instructions published elsewhere in this offer.

DREAM COME TRUE SWEEPSTAKES

Sweepstakes begins 9/1/94, ends 1/15/96. To qualify for the Early Bird Prize, entry must be received by the date specified elsewhere in this offer. Winners will be selected in random drawings on 2/29/96 by an independent judging organization whose decisions are final. Early Bird winner will be selected in a separate drawing from among all qualifying entries.

Odds of winning determined by total number of entries received. Distribution not to exceed 300 million.

Estimated maximum retail value of prizes: Grand (1) $25,000 (cash alternative $20,000); First (1) $2,000; Second (1) $750; Third (50) $75; Fourth (1,000) $50; Early Bird (1) $5,000. Total prize value: $86,500.

Automobile and travel trailer must be picked up at a local dealer; all other merchandise prizes will be shipped to winners. Awarding of any prize to a minor will require written permission of parent/guardian. If a trip prize is won by a minor, s/he must be accompanied by parent/legal guardian. Trip prizes subject to availability and must be completed within 12 months of date awarded. Blackout dates may apply. Early Bird trip is on a space available basis and does not include port charges, gratuities, optional shore excursions and onboard personal purchases. Prizes are not transferable or redeemable for cash except as specified. No substitution for prizes except as necessary due to unavailability. Travel trailer and/or automobile license and registration fees are winners' responsibility as are any other incidental expenses not specified herein.

Early Bird Prize may not be offered in some presentations of this sweepstakes. Grand through third prize winners will have the option of selecting any prize offered at level won. All prizes will be awarded. Drawing will be held at 204 Center Square Road, Bridgeport, NJ 08014. Winners need not be present. For winners list (available in June, 1996), send a self-addressed, stamped envelope by 1/15/96 to: Dream Come True Winners, P.O. Box 572, Gibbstown, NJ 08027.

THE FOLLOWING APPLIES TO THE SWEEPSTAKES ABOVE:

No purchase necessary. No photocopied or mechanically reproduced entries will be accepted. Not responsible for lost, late, misdirected, damaged, incomplete, illegible, or postage-die mail. Entries become the property of sponsors and will not be returned.

Winner(s) will be notified by mail. Winner(s) may be required to sign and return an affidavit of eligibility/release within 14 days of date on notification or an alternate may be selected. Except where prohibited by law, entry constitutes permission to use of winners' names, hometowns, and likenesses for publicity without additional compensation. Void where prohibited or restricted. All federal, state, provincial, and local laws and regulations apply.

All prize values are in U.S. currency. Presentation of prizes may vary; values at a given prize level will be approximately the same. All taxes are winners' responsibility.

Canadian residents, in order to win, must first correctly answer a time-limited skill testing question administered by mail. Any litigation regarding the conduct and awarding of a prize in this publicity contest by a resident of the province of Quebec may be submitted to the Regie des loteries et courses du Quebec.

Sweepstakes is open to legal residents of the U.S., Canada, and Europe (in those areas where made available) who have received this offer.

Sweepstakes in sponsored by Ventura Associates, 1211 Avenue of the Americas, New York, NY 10036 and presented by independent businesses. Employees of these, their advertising agencies and promotional companies involved in this promotion, and their immediate families, agents, successors, and assignees shall be ineligible to participate in the promotion and shall not be eligible for any prizes covered herein. SWP 3/95